HEAR THE WIND BLOW

MARY DOWNING HAHN

HEAR THE WIND BLOW

Clarion Books

NEW YORK

Clarion Books
a Houghton Mifflin Company imprint
215 Park Avenue South, New York, NY 10003
Copyright © 2003 by Mary Downing Hahn

The text was set in 11.5-point New Century Schoolbook.
Book design by Carol Goldenberg.

www.houghtonmifflinbooks.com

Printed in the U.S.A.

Library of Congress Cataloging-in-Publication Data

Hahn, Mary Downing.
Hear the wind blow / by Mary Downing Hahn.
p. cm.
Summary: With their mother dead and their home burned,
a thirteen-year-old boy and his little sister set out across Virginia
in search of relatives during the final days of the Civil War.
ISBN 0-618-18190-3 (alk. paper)
1. United States—History—Civil War, 1861-1865—Juvenile fiction.
[1. United States—History—Civil War, 1861-1865—Fiction. 2. Brothers
and sisters—Fiction. 3. Survival—Fiction. 4. Shenandoah River Valley
(Va. and W. Va.)—History—Civil War, 1861-1865—Fiction.] I. Title.
PZ7.H1256 He 2003
[Fic]—dc21
2002015977

QUM 10 9 8 7 6 5 4 3 2

FOR JEFF MOSS,
with thanks

———————————

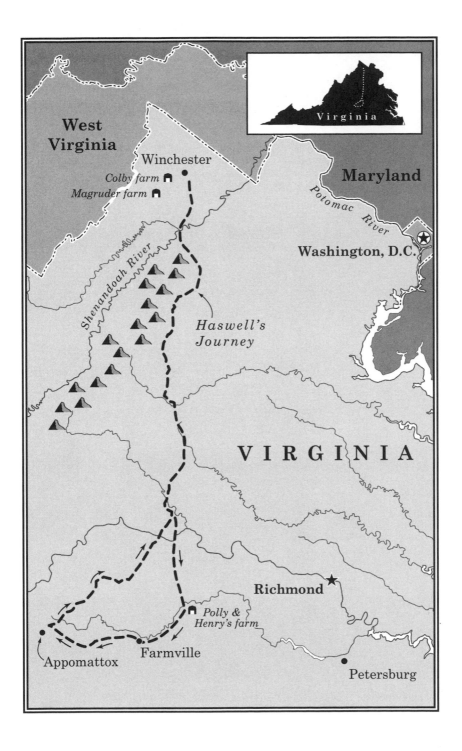

HEAR THE WIND BLOW

• 1 •

THE DAY THE SOLDIER rode up our lane, I was heading for the barn to milk the cow. It was late in the afternoon, almost dark, and just beginning to snow. The flakes spun idly, blowing this way and that, as if they were unsure where to settle.

I stopped and watched the soldier come closer. He sat crooked in the saddle, his head down, his body swaying in rhythm with the horse's slow steps. The snow sparkled like little gems on his shoulders and his hair.

Though both horse and rider looked too near death to be dangerous, I eyed the man uneasily. Folks here in the Shenandoah Valley had suffered many encounters with soldiers. Didn't matter if the armies were Confederate or Yankee. They both helped themselves to our food and our livestock. The only difference was the Confederates usually apologized for taking them. Unfortunately, words didn't ease our hunger.

What made the soldier especially menacing was the fact I was the only male standing between him and Mama and Rachel. Last year Papa had died in Richmond of dysentery. Not two months after Papa's body was sent home, my brother, Avery, rode off to join the army. Mama had begged him not to go, but he wanted to fight for the South, like Papa.

At the time, I was all for his going; I would have gone myself, but Mama clung to me with all her strength. Before Avery rode off on our one and only horse, he told me I was in charge of the farm till he returned.

The very last thing he said was, "You take good care of Mama and Rachel."

And that's just what I was trying to do. Protect Mama and Rachel from soldiers roaming the Valley like starving bears, looking to survive no matter what it might cost another person.

Even though my knees were trembly with fear, I stood and faced the soldier. "What do you want? Why don't you say something?"

He raised his head slowly and looked at me. His eyes were glassy, unfocused, his face deathly white under a layer of grime. Despite his beard and long hair, I could see he wasn't much older than Avery—eighteen, nineteen. Surely not over twenty.

My fear eased a bit, and I loosened my death grip on the milk bucket. "What do you want?" I asked again.

"Food," he croaked in a low voice. "And shelter . . . Please."

As quiet as he spoke, there was no mistaking his accent. He came from somewhere nearby. I dropped the milk bucket with a clang and ran to his side just in time to prevent him from sliding off the horse.

"Mama," I hollered toward the house. "Mama!"

The back door opened and my mother looked out, her thin face drawn tight with worry. My little sister, Rachel, peeked out from behind Mama's skirt. "Haswell," Mama called to me, "who's that with you?"

"Name's James Marshall," the man muttered. "Got shot a day or so ago. Lost a lot of blood."

I turned to Mama. "His name's James Marshall. He's wounded."

"Tell him to be on his way," Mama said. "We can't help him."

I was almost too shocked to speak. "But, Mama, he's hurt, he's—"

"You heard me, Haswell. I'm sorry, but he can't stay here." With that, Mama slammed the door. A second later Rachel's face appeared at the window, her nose pressed white against the glass.

I turned back to James Marshall. "Wait here. I'll talk to Mama. She has a kind heart, she'll—"

James Marshall sighed. "Can't blame her. I'll try somewhere else." He made as if to ride on, but the horse looked as near collapse as he did.

I grabbed the reins from him and glanced at the house. Rachel was gone from the window. There was no sign of Mama. The snow was falling thick now; it lay between us and the house like a heavy white curtain. Hoping not to be seen, I led the horse around to the back of the barn. It was cold and damp inside. What was left of the hay had a moldy smell. But it was better than being outside in the wind and cold.

I touched James Marshall's hand. "Lie down in the straw, and I'll fetch you some blankets."

He stared at me, his eyes glassier than before, and slid off the horse. I swear he was asleep before he hit the ground. The horse lay down beside him, its eyes closed, its breath steaming in the cold air. It was so skinny I could have counted its ribs. They were a pitiful pair.

I ran for a pile of old saddle blankets and covered James Marshall as best I could. Up close, he was a sad sight. His face was hollowed out with hunger and weariness, his beard and hair unkempt, his skin gray with dirt. Somehow I had to get food and drink to him and see to his wounds. If I didn't, he'd either freeze to death or die of an infection.

I milked the cow as fast as I could. She twitched her tail in my face and stamped her feet to show she wasn't used to such rough treatment. I rested my head against her warm flank and smelled the sweet milk filling the pail. Once, we'd had a whole herd of cows, but that was before the Yankee devil Sheridan and his men came to the Valley. Fortunately, I'd had enough sense to hide Clarissa and a few chickens in the gully behind our house. Otherwise, we'd have died of starvation before now.

"Poor old Clarissa," I told the cow, "you must be mighty lonesome."

She turned her head and looked at me with her sad brown eyes. Then she mooed, almost as if she'd understood what I'd said.

By the time I made my way to the house, the snow was even heavier and the sky was solid white. The wind blew across the yard. It looked like winter was throwing a February blizzard at us, a last insult after the bad weather we'd already been dealt. I was glad James Marshall wasn't still plodding along on his horse. He'd be a dead man by now, frozen stiff in the saddle.

Mama watched me set the milk on a shelf in the pantry. "Do you understand why I couldn't let that man stay here?" she asked.

"I guess you're scared the Yankees will burn the house down if they find out." I fidgeted with the milk pail to keep from looking her in the eye. Mama always knew when I was hiding something from her.

"That's exactly what happened to some folks down Haymarket way. They took in one of Mosby's men, and when the Yankees found out, they burned everything they couldn't steal. There's no one in the Valley they hate more than Mosby."

Mama turned away and went to the window. "Still, I can't help feeling bad about it," she said softly. "He was a young man and sorely wounded from the look of him. I reckon he'll die in this storm." She paused and gazed out the window as if she could see James Marshall out there succumbing to the cold.

"Maybe I shouldn't have turned him away," she added. "The sweet Lord knows I don't want his death on my conscience. Suppose someone let Avery die alone in the snow?"

Rachel looked up from her doll cradle. "Don't worry, Mama." Giving me a sly grin, she added, "I saw Haswell take that soldier around behind the barn. Most likely he's sleeping out there in the straw."

"Rachel!" When I took a step toward her, she jumped up and hid behind Mama's skirt, her favorite refuge.

"Haswell Colby Magruder," Mama said. "Is that the truth?"

"Yes, ma'am." I lowered my head and stared at the pine floor. "He would have died otherwise. There's blood on his jacket, and he's so weak he just about fell off the horse. Nobody will see him out in the barn. I'll tend him. You won't have to do a thing."

While Mama listened to the words tumbling out of my mouth, she looked at the wall of falling snow pressing against the kitchen window. The light whitened her face and showed a network of wrinkles radiating from her eyes. She looked old and tired, worn out from grief and want. I felt like hugging her the way I had when I was little, but at thirteen a boy doesn't hang on to his mother.

"I'm sorry, Mama, but he looked so pitiful, him and the horse both. I just couldn't turn him away. He's not much older than Avery and fighting for the same cause."

Mama laid her hand on my arm. "It's all right, son," she hushed me. "We'd best bring him inside and take proper care of him. With luck, no one will know he's been here." She glanced at Rachel, who was rocking her doll in its cradle but not missing a word we spoke. "You hear, Rachel? Don't tell a soul about that young man. Keep your mouth shut tight if anyone asks."

Rachel smiled—pleased, I reckon, to be included in something so important. At seven, she got left out of most serious matters. "You can trust me, Mama. I'm old enough to keep a secret."

While Rachel babbled on about how trustworthy she was, Mama pulled on her coat. "Come along, Haswell," she said. "I'll need your help getting the young man into the house."

"Can I come, too?" Rachel asked.

Mama sighed and opened the back door. Grabbing our coats, Rachel and I followed her through the thick snow to the barn. "Worst winter in years," Mama muttered. "Must be the Lord punishing us for this war."

I hated hearing Mama talk like that. You'd think she was a Quaker the way she carried on. But I kept my thoughts to myself and hoped she wouldn't speak ill of the fighting in James Marshall's hearing.

Mama knelt down and touched James Marshall's forehead. "Fever," she murmured. "Help me get him up on his feet, Haswell."

James Marshall opened his eyes and did his best to

stand, but it took all my strength and Mama's, too, to get him walking. Even then, he staggered between us, his arms around our shoulders, his head hanging. Rachel followed us out of the barn, claiming she'd catch him if he fell backward. Most likely she'd fall down in the snow with James Marshall on top of her, but I was working too hard to point this out.

Somehow we got James Marshall into the house and up the back stairs to the spare room over the kitchen. Once we'd had an Irish servant girl living there, cooking our meals and cleaning and laundering, but she'd run off with a Yankee soldier a year or so back.

Though Maura hadn't shown good judgment in her choice of a partner, I missed her. She made a good apple pie. I liked the soft way she spoke, too, and the stories she told about the fairies and such.

James Marshall fell across the narrow bed with a groan. After sending Rachel downstairs to start the kettle boiling, Mama began to undress him. I helped by pulling off his boots. They were made of fine leather but the soles were worn clean through. I thought of Avery's boots, so shiny and new when he left for the war. Did they look as bad as these now?

"Go down and fetch a bowl of hot water," Mama said. She'd peeled James Marshall's shirt away to reveal a wound in his side. "He's lost a lot of blood."

I glanced at the bloody shirt and coat and the hole in James Marshall's skin, all purple and red and ugly.

"And bring the bottle of whiskey from Papa's cabinet," she called after me.

I hurried to the kitchen. Rachel had gotten the kettle to boil, and I poured the steaming water in a bowl. She followed me upstairs with the whiskey.

Mama was tearing a clean sheet into strips. "Set the bowl on the table by the bed, Haswell. The whiskey, too."

I did as she told me, and she got to work cleaning the wound. James Marshall moaned and tossed, clearly out of his head by now.

"Hold his arms, Haswell," Mama ordered.

I did my best, but sick as the man was, he was strong. Somehow I managed to keep him still long enough for Mama to do her work. Using her fingers, she dug a bullet out of the wound and tossed it on the floor. Rachel and I stared at it. Like me, she was probably wondering how it felt to have something like that pierce your flesh.

Rachel stooped down and picked up the bullet, turning it in her fingers and studying it.

"Put that down," Mama said sharply.

"I want it." Rachel wiped it on her dress and dropped it in her pocket.

Mama was too busy tending James Marshall to do more than frown and shake her head. Before she bandaged him, she poured whiskey in the wound. He screamed in pain, and she held the bottle to his lips. "Drink some," she said, "but not too much."

Once Mama was through with him, James Marshall lay back and closed his eyes.

"Sit by him, Haswell," Mama said. "Give him a sip of whiskey if he wakes. I'll go down and fix something to fortify him."

Rachel stood close beside me, her breath warm on my neck. "You think he'll die?" she whispered.

"I hope not."

She studied James Marshall for a while. "He's real sick. Most likely he *will* die."

"Maybe you should go down and help Mama," I said.

—— 8 ——

"Remember when our cat Sadie died and we buried her in the orchard? Maybe we'll have to bury James Marshall, too. I can say the prayers, and you and Mama can sing the hymns."

"I sure hope he can't hear the things you're saying."

Rachel went to the window and peered out at the snow. "His tracks are all covered up already."

"Good."

Rachel breathed a big foggy patch on the glass and drew a picture of a cat with her finger. "Remember how sweet and pretty Sadie was?"

"Go on downstairs, Rachel."

She stuck out her tongue at me and turned back to the window. "I guess Sadie's nothing but bones by now," she said. "Dead and gone. You think she's waiting up in heaven, Haswell?"

"Hush up, Rachel," I hissed at her. "What kind of talk is that? Cats don't go to heaven."

Before Rachel could come up with a sassy answer, James Marshall groaned and opened his eyes. They were all sparkly bright, burning with fever like blue fire. "Where am I?"

He was trying to sit up, so I eased him back on the pillow and gave him a sip of whiskey. "It's all right," I said. "You're safe in our house. Mama took pity on you. She's downstairs now, fixing a concoction for you."

"It'll taste horrid," Rachel put in. "But it will make you better, so maybe you won't die after all."

James Marshall stared at Rachel as if she were a creature of ill omen. "Who are you?"

"I'm Rachel Magruder," she said. "I'm seven years old and I'm the best speller in my school. I can count to one hundred and I know my times tables up to the fives. I can read long books, too. The Bible, for instance. And I—"

I put my hand over her mouth. "Hush, Rachel. James Marshall doesn't want to hear your entire life story."

Rachel pulled away. "Don't you do that again, Haswell, or I'm telling Mama." She turned back to James Marshall. "My brother is the rudest boy in the whole state of Virginia. And he has smelly hands."

"Why don't you go see if Mama needs you?" I asked her.

"Why don't you?" Rachel said in the snippy voice she loved to use on me.

"Well, aren't you the pert little miss," James Marshall observed.

If I hadn't been taught to be polite, I might have called Rachel something worse than pert. As it was, I just scowled at her. She had been a contrary child since the day she was born. Did and said what she pleased, and the devil take those who didn't like it. Papa said she was the spitting image of Grandma Colby, Mama's mama. He didn't intend it as a compliment.

Rachel smiled at James Marshall. "Want to see something?"

Before he could say yes or no, Rachel opened her hand and showed him the bullet, still slimy with blood. "Mama dug this out of your side. Did it hurt going in?"

James Marshall nodded. "It most certainly did."

Just as I was about to lose my control and say something rude to Rachel, Mama came upstairs carrying a steaming cup of foul-smelling liquid. I don't know what went into it—herbs and such, I reckon. She gathered the makings in the summer and hung bunches of weeds in the attic to dry. In the fall she brewed it in a kettle, poured it into bottles, and called it medicine. Poison, more likely. At least that's how it tasted.

Mama sat down on the bed. "Did these children wake you, son?"

James Marshall shook his head. "I'm in some pain, ma'am."

Mama held the cup toward him. "Drink this. It will help with the fever. And the pain."

Rachel wrinkled her nose. "Poor James Marshall," she said without a trace of pity. "If you hold your nose while you drink it, you won't smell it."

James Marshall ignored Rachel and did his best to choke down Mama's remedy. I could tell by his face it tasted just as bad as usual. When he handed Mama the empty cup, Rachel gave him a long, admiring look.

"I never have managed to swallow more than one mouthful of that concoction," she admitted. "Usually I just spit it out."

James Marshall coughed and closed his eyes. Mama smoothed his covers and studied his face. "What a handsome young man." She sighed long and heavy. "Most likely his mother is worried sick about him at this very moment."

The wind thumped the windows as she spoke, shaking the glass as if it meant to break into the room. I knew Mama was thinking about Avery again. We needed him so badly, it made me hate him sometimes. Why had he left me to take care of everything, and me just thirteen years old? When he came home, I'd tell him a thing or two.

"Can you take Rachel to the kitchen and feed her some of that stew?" Mama asked me. "I want to sit here a spell and watch this poor young man."

Rachel fussed a bit, but she followed me downstairs and seated herself at the table. I ladled possum stew into two bowls and sat down opposite her. I'd caught the varmint myself in one of Papa's traps, and I was mighty pleased with the way Mama had cooked him up.

Except for the wind howling around the house, the room was quiet. And warm from the fire in the woodstove. I was glad I'd collected a good pile of logs before the storm commenced.

After a while Rachel put down her spoon and leaned toward me, her face scrunched in worry. "Do you think the Yankees are searching for him?"

"I hope not."

Rachel turned to the window. Dark was falling fast and we could see our reflections in the glass, Rachel in her pigtails and me with my hair hanging in my eyes. Behind us, the kitchen looked snug and safe, yellow with lamplight.

"They could be out there in the dark right now," Rachel whispered, "watching us."

As she spoke, the wind hit the house hard, driving cold air through every crack. Rachel and I both shivered, partly from the draft and partly from fear. Suddenly, the kitchen didn't seem so safe after all.

"Those Federals won't go anywhere in this snow," I told her. "They're huddled around their campfires somewhere faraway, waiting for spring to recommence fighting."

"I've heard tell the Yankees are demons from hell," Rachel said. "Maybe they can follow a man by his smell, like the devil can."

Even though Rachel was merely a child, she was beginning to scare the beejeebers out of me. Hadn't I heard older folks say the same thing about the Yankees? I scraped the last bit of gravy out of my bowl and got to my feet. "Let's take Mama some stew and then go to bed," I said. "We'll be warm and snug under the blankets."

For once Rachel agreed with me. I carried the bowl of

stew upstairs, and she followed with a chunk of bread. Mama was sitting in the rocker beside the bed. Even though James Marshall had swallowed every drop of her remedy, he still looked mighty sick to me.

"We brought you something to eat," Rachel told Mama.

Mama smiled at us. "Set it down on the bureau," she said. "I'll eat it later."

Rachel drew closer to Mama. "Is he getting any better?" she whispered.

Mama sighed. "He's no worse, thank the Lord."

"Is he fixing to die?" Rachel asked.

Mama hushed her. "Go on to bed, child."

We did as Mama said. Long after Rachel fell asleep, I lay awake, listening to the wind, thinking what a scary sound it made. Like the souls of the dead out there in the cold and the dark, wailing to be in their beds again, warm and snug. I pictured Avery sleeping in a tent somewhere, huddled under his blankets. And men like James Marshall alone and wandering the night like lost souls themselves. And officers in snug shelters, planning battles and dreaming of glory.

I fell asleep thinking I might ride away with James Marshall when he recovered. I'd find Avery and bring him home and make him do his share to protect Mama and Rachel. We needed him a sight more than General Robert E. Lee did.

◦ 2 ◦

I WOKE TO A COLD, gray dawn and went down the hall to check on James Marshall. Mama was asleep in the chair beside the bed, looking weary even in repose, but James Marshall was awake. He raised his hand to signify he saw me, and I crept close to him.

"How are you feeling?" I whispered.

"Poorly," he murmured, "but better than yesterday."

Even though we'd kept our voices low, Mama's eyes opened. She always did sleep as light as a cat. Leaning toward James Marshall, she laid a hand on his forehead. "Still feverish," she said, "but not near as hot as last night. My remedy must be helping."

James Marshall smiled. "I surely hope so, ma'am, for that is without a doubt the worst concoction I ever swallowed."

Mama's face brightened. "Only a man who's recovering complains about the taste of things." She turned to me. "Go on and get the stove fired up for cooking, Haswell."

"And see to my horse, please," James Marshall added.

I glanced at Mama and she nodded. "Tend to the horse first. And see to Clarissa."

When I opened the kitchen door, the wind hit me hard. The snow had stopped, but it lay mighty deep, especially the drifts against the side of the barn. It was hard work crossing the yard. The horse was on his feet, looking better. I fed him some oats leftover from our own horses and draped a blanket over his back. While he ate, I stroked his neck and whispered to him, for he'd been ridden hard and needed some extra comforting. He was a good horse, a black gelding with fine legs and a handsome face. Intelligent, I thought. And loyal. Not the sort of horse we'd ever owned. We were farmers, and our horses had to work the fields and pull wagons.

After I fed Clarissa, I walked back to the house, thinking about James Marshall and his family. It could be they were wealthy, owning a fine horse like that. Or it could be he stole the horse from the Yankees.

While I was feeding the fire in the kitchen, Rachel came downstairs. "James Marshall's feeling better, Mama claims, though he doesn't look real good to me. Most ashy-faced man I ever did see."

Without expecting an answer, she went to the window and peered out. "Just look at all that snow, Haswell. It's the most I've seen in my whole entire life. If James Marshall hadn't come to our house, both him and his horse would be dead and buried in it."

"You are positively the most morbid-minded child in the state of Virginia," I said.

"What's that mean?" Rachel looked offended that I knew a word she didn't.

"Morbid? It means you're always thinking gloomy thoughts about death and dying."

Rachel smiled. "Morbid," she repeated, "*moooor-bid*. It has the saddest sound. Don't you just love words that sound like what they mean?"

I poked the fire. "I've never thought about that."

Rachel stuck out her tongue, her usual response, and picked up her doll. "Oh, Sophia," she crooned, "did you know you have a *moooor-bid* mama?"

Our mama came down then and told me to go up and sit with James Marshall a spell while she fixed breakfast. Rachel started to follow me, but Mama told her to stay and give her a hand with the oatmeal. Silently I thanked the Lord for small favors.

James Marshall was awake. He had the sharpest blue eyes I ever saw, but they weren't burning bright with fever this morning. "Did you see to my horse?" he asked.

"I did, and he's looking a sight better than you."

James Marshall smiled. "I'm glad to hear that."

"He's a mighty fine horse," I said.

"He is indeed. I call him Warrior. I've had him since I was about your age. He was my thirteenth-birthday present."

"That was a grand gift." I spoke with some envy. My thirteenth birthday had come and gone without much notice, like most of the ones before it.

"Papa has a horse farm south of here, not far from Harrisonburg. He breeds horses. Or he did before the war. Most of his herd was taken by the army, both North and South."

James Marshall lay back on his pillow and gazed at the ceiling. "As soon as I'm strong enough, I'll be on my way. I don't want to bring the Yankees here."

"Were they following you?"

"I think I lost them. We all scattered after the raid. That bullet slowed me down, but I had good cover in the woods. They didn't see which way I went. Probably thought I was dead." He paused a moment, as if he were contemplating his close call with eternity. "Is your father in the fighting?"

"Papa served under General Stonewall Jackson himself till Chancellorsville." I tugged at a feather poking out of the quilt, suddenly conscious of the voices in the wind howling outside in the cold. Somehow it seemed shameful to tell James Marshall that Papa had died from dysentery. I was tempted to lie and say he'd been killed in battle, a hero. So I shifted the subject somewhat.

"Papa was one of the guards who took Stonewall to Guinea Station after he lost his arm. He was there when Stonewall died."

"That was a great loss," James Marshall said softly. "The South never had a finer general than Stonewall Jackson."

"Did you hear what Stonewall said before he died?" I asked.

James Marshall nodded. "His last words were, 'Let us cross the river and rest in the shade of the trees.' People say he looked as if he really saw the river and the trees instead of the bedroom wall."

"Papa said it was the River Jordan he saw. Is that what you think?"

"Most certainly. All of us will cross it one day and rest in the shade." James Marshall looked out the window at the bare trees shivering in the wind. He turned back to me, his blue eyes searching my face. "Will you do something for me, Haswell?"

"Of course." Though I didn't feel comfortable saying it, I'd do anything he asked me.

"There's a letter in my pocket." He pointed to his greatcoat, which Mama had hung on the back of a chair. "It's addressed to my father. If I die of this wound, promise you'll see he receives it."

"You won't die," I said, "but I'll promise anyway."

"Go and get it," he said. "Keep it safe."

I reached into his coat pockets reluctantly. Even though he'd told me to do it, it seemed like stealing somehow. I pulled out a dirty, ragged envelope and held it up so he could see. "Is this it?"

James Marshall nodded and held out his hand for the letter. He studied it and gave it back. "I guess the postman will be able to read my handwriting."

He watched me slide the envelope into my pants pocket. I thought he might want to sleep, but when I headed for the door, he stopped me. "Sit down, Haswell. You never did finish telling me about your father."

It seemed I hadn't distracted James Marshall after all. I settled on the quilt and tugged at that same old feather. "Papa died in Richmond while he was on guard duty. They sent his unit there after Chancellorsville—you know, to give them a rest." I paused and added, "After all the fighting he saw, he went and died of dysentery."

"Now that's a shame." James Marshall shook his head. "Your poor mama. She's got you and your sister to take care of. And a farm as well. Can't be easy for her."

"When the war's over, my brother, Avery, will come home and help me with the farm. He ran off to join the war not long after Papa died."

"Do you know where is he now?"

"He's been at Petersburg since last summer when the siege began. Every now and then he manages to send us a letter."

"From what I hear, that's a bad place to be and mighty hard to get out of. Folks there have come to eating dogs, cats, rats, just about anything."

"Avery says they eat what they can get," I muttered. "The Yankees have cut off everything. Nothing goes in, nothing goes out."

"It's a cruel war." James Marshall glanced at me. "How old is your brother?"

"Avery's sixteen, just three years older than I am."

"That's how old I was when I left home to fight with Mosby's men."

"You're with Mosby?" I stared at him with awe. John Singleton Mosby was the smartest man in Virginia, and the boldest. There was nothing he couldn't get away with. Horses, food, ammunition. Why, that man could walk right into a Northern camp and leave with whatever he fancied, and none the wiser till he was safely away.

James Marshall smiled. "Everything you hear about that wily fox is true. That's why I joined his Rangers."

"Best not tell Mama who you ride with," I said. "The Yankees hate Mosby. She's already scared of what they'll do to us if they find you here."

He nodded as if he understood. For a while we sat together quietly, listening to the wind. "The truth is, Mama doesn't care which side wins anymore," I said. "I heard her say so herself. She just wants the killing to stop. And Avery to come home safe."

James Marshall frowned. "The South is worth fighting for. Even dying for. We can't have Yankees telling us what to do. Doesn't your mama understand that?"

"Well, you know how ladies are. They don't appreciate the art of war." I pulled so hard at the feather it came out of the quilt. Mama would have slapped my hand if she'd seen what I'd done. Good thing she was still rattling pans in the kitchen and fussing at Rachel.

"Least that's what Papa said," I went on. "He tried and tried to explain old-time heroes like Achilles and Alexander the Great and Horatio, but Mama wasn't interested in their deeds. She said the world doesn't need any more heroes. According to her, we'd all be better off if men stayed home and minded their own patch."

James Marshall smiled at that and so did I, for it was funny to picture the heroes of history plowing fields or hoeing gardens, living to be old and gray. A man didn't win fame and glory that way.

"Do you know your Homer?" James Marshall asked.

I nodded. "Papa was a scholarly man. He read the *Iliad* and the *Odyssey* to Avery and me. Then when I got smarter, I read them myself. Avery, too. In fact, the two of us used to act out battle scenes. Avery always got to be Achilles because he was older and his name started with *A*. I had to be Hector. *H* for Hector, you know. Avery got to kill me every single time."

James Marshall coughed to clear his throat. "Do you recall what Achilles said before he went into battle?"

I nodded. "He knew he'd die if he fought; it was his destiny. But he decided he'd rather die a hero in battle than live out his life and die safe in his bed."

James Marshall nodded. "Heroes' names are remembered forever," he added, "but an old man's name is soon forgotten."

Mama had come upstairs while we were talking. James Marshall didn't see her, but I did. From the look on her face, I knew she hated what we were saying.

"If you aim to have a long life, you should be resting,

James Marshall," Mama said sternly. "Not talking your fool head off."

"Now, now, Mrs. Magruder, I was paraphrasing Homer himself, a man we all esteem."

"Try reading your Bible instead," Mama said. "Ecclesiastes, for instance. 'For to him that is joined to all the living there is hope: for a living dog is better than a dead lion.'"

Before James Marshall could come up with a rejoinder, Mama stuck a spoonful of her medicine into his mouth. That silenced him from giving his opinion of dead lions and living dogs. But I knew he didn't agree with Ecclesiastes. Or Mama, either.

As for myself, I wasn't sure. I wanted to believe in the glory of war, but so far all I'd seen was soldiers burning farms and stealing food from folks who needed it just as badly as they did. Maybe you had to be in the actual fighting to see what Homer saw. Papa hadn't said much about his experiences, but I was certain Avery would have plenty to tell me.

"Don't just stand there dreaming, Haswell," Mama said. "Go on downstairs and do something useful. Shovel a path to the barn." She didn't sound cross. Just firm. But as I left the room, I heard her mutter, "Damn Homer and his foolishness."

I'd never heard Mama say damn anything so I figured she must be angrier than I'd realized.

◇

The wind had dropped and the snow lay thick and white over the fields, carved into banks and drifts and hollows. The sun stood at the top of the blue sky, shining so bright it dazzled my eyes. Lord, it was a pretty sight. But it didn't make the shoveling any easier.

When I went into the barn to tend the cow and Warrior, I could scarcely see. Snow-blind, I guessed. The horse raised his head and whinnied, as if to say he wanted his oats and he wanted them now. I fed him and visited with him a while.

"Don't worry. Your master's on the mend already," I told him. "He'll be down to see you in no time."

Warrior seemed to understand every word I spoke. I'd never known a horse to look so intelligent. I reckoned he was the equal of Alexander the Great's noble steed Bucephalus in looks as well as brains.

By the time I returned to the house with a bucket of milk, Mama was busy kneading bread and Rachel was drawing pictures on the steamy kitchen windows. The air smelled as sweet as a field of mown wheat on a hot summer day.

I stamped my feet to warm them and rubbed my hands together. "How's James Marshall?"

"Sleeping," Mama said. "His wound is healing nicely. Wasn't near as bad as it looked. His fever's down, too. I believe what he needed most was warmth and nourishment and sleep."

That was good news. I had half a mind to sneak up and take a peek at him. If he was awake, I planned to ask him what getting shot was like, and had he been scared, and did he ever have a chance to sit down next to Mosby and talk to him close up. But the second I put my foot on the step, Mama shook her head.

"Leave the poor boy alone, Haswell. Didn't I just say rest is what he needs?"

"Yes, ma'am." I headed for the parlor to find a book to read, but Rachel got there first.

"Read to me, Haswell." She thrust *Great Expectations* at me. Papa was very fond of Mr. Dickens and had acquired most of his books, including this one, the very latest. He'd managed to find a copy in Richmond and brought it home for Christmas. He'd read the entire book to us, sitting by the fire on cold winter nights.

It was simpler to read to Rachel than argue with her, so I took the book and began at the beginning, even though we both knew the story almost by heart. Pip's meeting with the convict in the foggy graveyard always gave me the shivers. Sometimes I lay awake wondering what I'd do if I ever experienced a moment like that.

"'Hold your noise!'" I read. "'Keep still, you little devil, or I'll cut your throat!'"

I did my best to speak with expression the way Papa did, but I couldn't make the convict's voice sound as gruff as he could.

"A fearful man," I read on, "all in coarse grey, with a great iron on his leg. A man with no hat, and with broken shoes, and with an old rag tied round his head. A man who had been soaked in water, and smothered in mud, and lamed by stones, and cut by flints, and stung by nettles, and torn by briars; who limped and shivered, and glared and growled; and whose teeth chattered in his head as he seized me by the chin.

"'O! Don't cut my throat, sir,' I pleaded in terror."

Now I pitched my voice higher, imitating poor scared Pip. Beside me, Rachel listened hard. You'd think she'd never heard the story before.

"The convict sounds like a Yankee," she whispered. "They'd just as soon cut our throats as not."

"That would hush a person, wouldn't it?"

Rachel didn't catch my meaning. "What will we do if they come here searching for James Marshall, Haswell?"

"They won't."

"But what if they do?"

"Do you want to hear Mr. Dickens or fret about Yankees?"

Rachel leaned up against me. "Read, Haswell."

So the afternoon passed. While we followed Pip's adventures, the sky darkened slowly. Soon it was time to feed Warrior and milk the cow.

When my chores were done, I took a bowl of soup to James Marshall. He was sitting up in bed looking a world better, but his eyes had dark shadows and his skin was still white as milk that's had the cream skimmed off.

"Tell me about getting shot in the raid," I said.

He shrugged. "Not much to tell, Haswell." He spooned soup into his mouth.

"That's all right," I said. "Tell it anyway. Papa never would say a thing about fighting."

"Maybe he had cause not to." James Marshall glanced at me and went on eating the soup.

"But is it like Homer tells it? Full of blood and noise and heads rolling on the ground?"

"Yes, I guess it is."

"And glory? And heroes?"

James Marshall put his soup spoon down and stared at me. "Haswell, I didn't see much glory. Plenty of blood, plenty of noise, plenty of heads rolling on the ground. But not much glory."

"But heroes? There were heroes?"

"Yes, I did see heroes." He stirred his soup slowly, lifting the spoon and watching the liquid slop back into the bowl. "But most of them died."

I sighed. "Like Achilles."

"Yes," James Marshall agreed. "Short lives full of bravery."

"But you still haven't told me how you got wounded," I reminded him.

"We raided a Yankee camp and stole some horses. Just as we were leaving, three Yankees came riding up. We pretended to be Yankees ourselves and called out friendly greetings. We would have fooled them entirely if that poor fool Peter Jenks hadn't lost his nerve and fired off a shot. Next thing, they were shooting and we were shooting. They killed Peter and wounded William Pickens and me. I don't know what happened to William. I rode one way, and he must have gone another."

"I wish I could go with you when you leave here," I blurted out. "I'm thirteen—that's old enough to ride with you."

"Take my word for it, Haswell, a boy your age is better off at home." James Marshall finished the last of his soup and handed me the empty bowl. "Your mama needs you more than Mosby does."

It wasn't the answer I'd hoped to hear, but James Marshall was through talking. He lay back and closed his eyes.

I sat and watched him sleep. Sometimes he looked agitated, as if he were dreaming something bad. He ground his teeth, which made an awful noise. Once in a while he'd moan or groan. Then he'd thrash around, as if he were trying to escape from something. I wondered if he was getting any rest at all.

◇

When I went to bed that night, I lit my candle and studied James Marshall's envelope. It was addressed to Mr. Cecil

Montgomery Marshall, River View, Harrisonburg, Virginia. I wanted to open it and read the letter, but I knew that would be wrong. I put it back into my pants pocket and prayed the Lord would spare James Marshall's life so I would not have to send the letter to his father.

· 3 ·

A WEEK PASSED. By the end of it, James Marshall was up on his feet and tottering around the house, growing stronger every day. Mama fussed over him as if he were her son. She wanted him to stay till spring, and in truth he seemed in no hurry to depart. For one thing, the weather was still bad. Snow and sleet and ice storms made the roads almost impassable. No news came our way, no letters, no visits. Mosby could have been lying low in the Blue Ridge or stealing supplies from Yankee trains toward the East. It didn't make sense for James Marshall to ride off in search of the Rangers. They didn't call John Singleton Mosby the Gray Ghost for nothing.

During those dreary winter days and nights, James Marshall did his best to amuse. He teased Mama and made her laugh, something she hadn't done since Avery departed to win glory in battle. He pulled Rachel's braids and got away with it. That amazed me, for Rachel was not one to tolerate pranks. I suppose he won her heart by reading to her whenever she asked. He obliged me by telling amazing stories of Mosby's exploits. Soon we all looked upon him as a member of our family, a long-lost cousin who'd come to stay with us.

One stormy night, we were huddled around the stove listening to James Marshall tell of the time Mosby kidnapped a Yankee general out of his bed with Federals all over the place. They took a bunch of soldiers prisoner, stole fifty-eight horses as well, and got away without losing a single Ranger. He told the story so well Mama laughed, which gladdened my heart.

"How about a song, Mrs. Magruder?" James Marshall asked.

Mama smiled and blushed. "Oh, I haven't played or sung for such a long time. Surely you don't want your ears to ring with pain from my efforts."

"Now, Mrs. Magruder, I can't allow you to be so modest." James Marshall rose to his feet and offered Mama his hand. "Please." He bowed like a true gentleman. Mama's face reddened even more.

Rachel leapt up and clapped her hands. "Yes, Mama, yes! Please play and sing for us like you used to!"

Mama glanced at me. "Please, Mama," I begged. "You sing so beautifully."

Still blushing, Mama allowed us to lead her to the little organ in the parlor. She seated herself and opened one of Mr. Stephen Foster's song books. "What would you like to hear?"

"Play 'Jeanie with the Light Brown Hair,'" Rachel begged. "It's my very favorite song."

Mama smiled at her. "That's because you have light brown hair, just like Jeanie."

Rachel smoothed her braids and darted a coy look at James Marshall. If she'd been ten years older, I'd have thought she was flirting.

"It's also because you're morbid," I told her crossly. "You just love songs and books where people die." Turning to

Mama, I said, "Why can't we have a happy song like 'Oh! Susanna' or 'Camptown Races'?"

"Jeanie doesn't die," Rachel said, "She floats like a vapor, on the soft summer air."

"When did you ever see a live person float on the air?" I asked her.

Mama laid her hand on my arm. "That's enough, Haswell. I'll play 'Jeanie' first, and then you can pick a song."

As Mama struck the opening chords, Rachel made a little sneaky face at me. I might have made one back, but Mama began to sing. Her voice was so sweet, it brought tears to our eyes, especially at the end when she sang, "'Oh! I sigh for Jeanie with the light brown hair. Floating, like a vapor, on the soft summer air.'"

"Now 'Camptown Races,'" I said, but James Marshall said I should let Mama pick some pretty songs first. "Play your favorites, ma'am."

Mama smiled and turned to "Beautiful Dreamer." After that she picked "Come Where My Love Lies Dreaming," "I Would Not Die in Spring Time," and "Old Dog Tray." She finished up with "Hard Times Come Again No More."

Let us pause in life's pleasures and count its many tears
While we all sup sorrow with the poor;
There's a song that will linger forever in our ears;
Oh! Hard Times, come again no more.

It was a melancholy song, one Papa dismissed as overly sentimental, but the words always struck my heart, especially now when it seemed hard times had come to stay. While Mama sang, Rachel leaned against her; the lamplight touched their hair with gold. It was a perfect picture, one I knew I'd see in my mind's eye all my life.

By the time we reached the last chorus, we were the saddest folks you ever did see.

'Tis the song, the sigh of the weary;
Hard Times, Hard Times, come again no more.
Many days you have lingered around my cabin door;
Oh! Hard Times, come again no more.

As the last note faded away, Mama sighed and folded her hands in her lap. Tears sparkled in her eyes.

James Marshall laid his hand gently on her shoulder. "Perhaps we should hear 'Camptown Races' now," he suggested.

Mama wiped her eyes with her lacy handkerchief. "Yes," she agreed. "Burton loved that song." She glanced at Papa's tintype on the mantel, showing him in his uniform and beard, and then bent over the keyboard.

As soon as the song began, we all joined in. Our spirits lifted at once. We sang "Oh! Susanna" next, and then James Marshall himself took over the organ and played a grand medley of lively songs, including "Old Dan Tucker," "Cumberland Gap," and "The Bonnie Blue Flag."

Suddenly, Rachel flung her arms around him. "Oh, James Marshall," she cried, "stay with us forever. We haven't had so much merriment since Papa's last Christmas at home."

She turned to Mama and me. "Remember, Haswell? Remember, Mama? Papa was here, and Avery, too, and we were all singing round the organ, just like now."

James Marshall laughed. "Forever's a long time, Miss Rachel." With that, he launched into "Dixie."

He hadn't played more than a few notes when we heard a noise outside. At first we all thought it was the wind thudding against the house, but then we realized someone was pounding on the door.

Mama clutched Rachel tight. James Marshall froze at the keyboard. I stood by the organ, clutching the top. We didn't speak. We didn't move. No civilized person would pound on a door like that. It was the Yankees, coming to ruin everything.

James Marshall was the first to move. Rising to his feet, he ran upstairs as light-footed as a cat.

Mama grabbed my arm. "Look out the window, Haswell," she whispered. "Tell me what you see."

Cautiously I twitched the curtain aside and peered out. "Three men on horseback in the yard," I told her.

Then a voice hollered, "This is Captain Powell of the Pennsylvania Cavalry! Open up!"

Mama looked as if she might faint dead away. "Go to the door, Haswell. Give me time to compose myself." Turning to Rachel, she whispered, "Not one word about James Marshall."

I walked down the hall and slowly opened the front door. A man towered above me, a dark shape against the stormy sky. Frozen rain clung to his hair, his beard, and the shoulders of his greatcoat.

Pushing past me, he strode into the house, his three companions close behind. "What's your name, boy?"

"Haswell Colby Magruder." I stood as tall as I could and looked him in the eye without flinching. I'd never been this close to a Yankee, but I was damned if I was going to let on I was scared half dead.

"Where's your father?" he asked.

I hesitated. The captain was a fearsome ugly man. If I

told him Papa was dead, he'd know we had no one to protect us. There was no telling what he'd do then.

Before I'd had a chance to come up with an answer, Mama walked slowly toward us. Rachel clung to her skirt. "What do you want from us, sir?" she asked in a shaking voice. "Food, shelter?"

Captain Powell stepped closer to Mama. "We're looking for a Rebel, ma'am, one of Mosby's Bushwhackers. Rumor has it he came this way about three weeks ago, wounded. You seen him?"

Mama looked him straight in the eye. "No, sir. No one's come by here since the last snowfall."

The captain turned to Rachel. "What about you, sweetheart? You know a young man named James Marshall?"

Rachel shook her head.

"What's the matter, honey?" He reached for Rachel and tried to draw her away from Mama. "You ain't scared of me, are you?" He smiled at her. "I got a little daughter at home just as pretty as you."

Rachel shook her head and looked the captain in the eye. "I'm not afraid of you or any Yankees. Not even General Ulysses S. Grant himself."

The captain laughed. "Well, ain't you a cocky little thing." He glanced at Mama. "Is your mother as full of spirit as you are?" There was a look in his eye I didn't like, but I couldn't say why.

Captain Powell turned to his men. They straightened up as best they could, for they were a ragged group. The smell of them filled the hall. It got worse as they warmed up. Wet wool, dirty hair, dirty skin—I don't know what all.

"Search the house," the captain said. "You, Hicks, don't

just stand there looking stupid. Go on upstairs with Andrews."

Hicks was the smallest of the bunch, the youngest, too. He looked more scared than mean, but I reckoned he was just as nasty-natured as the rest. While he climbed the steps behind Andrews, the other man went to the back of the house. Their boots stamped about everywhere. The captain stayed in the hall, smoothing his beard and studying us.

Drawing Rachel and me close, Mama held our hands so tight my bones ached. We all feared for James Marshall's life. Not even Mosby himself could have gotten out of this situation.

"Where's your husband, Mrs. Magruder?" Captain Powell stepped a little closer to Mama, still with that look in his eye.

My skin crawled with fear and anger, but I had no idea what to do. Cursing myself for being a coward, I edged closer to Mama, hoping to protect her from the captain and the evil in his eyes. Rachel kept a hold of Mama's hand, but she glared at the Yankee.

Before Mama could answer the captain's question, Hicks gave a shout. "He's getting away, sir!"

At the moment he yelled, I heard hoofbeats. Then breaking glass upstairs and a volley of shots.

Mama clutched Rachel and me even tighter. Though we didn't look at one another, we all thought a miracle had happened. Somehow James Marshall had gotten to the barn and was riding away on Warrior. Surely he was safe now.

Hicks came running down the stairs so fast he tripped and slid into the hallway on his backside. Leaping to his feet, he said, "Captain, he got out a window and down a tree, sir."

"Did you hit him?"

"No, sir, not in the rain and the dark. He's gone."

Captain Powell scowled. "Get mounted, all of you, and go after him!"

The men made a rush for the door. "You coming, Captain?" Andrews asked.

"Somebody's got to keep an eye on the prisoners," he said.

Mama squeezed Rachel's and my hands. She didn't look at the captain. I had a feeling she was praying hard, so I did the same. Surely the merciful God in heaven wouldn't let us come to harm, for we worshiped every Sunday and did our best to obey His word. Not that I always succeeded, but on the whole I lived a good life and stayed out of the worst kinds of trouble. Hardly ever cursed. Only smoked once, just to see what it was like. Never took even a sip of whiskey. Read the Bible every night. Said my prayers.

While I was checking my conscience, Captain Powell looked at Mama and said, "You know there are penalties for sheltering a Rebel, ma'am, especially one of Mosby's thieving rats."

Mama held up her head and looked him straight in the eye, but she said nothing. She reminded me of a picture at Grandma Colby's house that showed Liberty as a tall, queenly lady, full of courage. I was mighty proud of her.

"Reprisals," the captain went on, "approved by General Meade his very self."

When Mama said nothing, he looked around the hall

and beyond, into the parlor. "Mighty nice home you have here. Clean, well kept, snug. Quality furnishings."

He went into the parlor. Drawing his sword, he brandished it at the chairs before the fireplace. Mama's and Papa's chairs, we'd always called them, for no one else was ever allowed to sit in them, though Rachel had sneaked her fanny into them more than once. The sword made a swishing sound in the air, but the captain didn't touch even the tip to the chairs.

Mama drew in her breath and bit her lip. I could feel the anger trembling through her body, but she stood just as tall and silent as ever.

"Pictures of your parents, I suppose." He pointed his sword at the paintings over the mantel, swishing it like he'd done before. If Grandma Colby had seen him do that, she'd have scratched his eyes out. No one showed *her* portrait disrespect.

"Pretty little china doodads—worth quite a bit, I reckon." He nudged Mama's precious shepherds and shepherdesses, the porcelain vase she treasured, and a variety of small pieces, some of which had belonged to her mother and grandmother before her.

Still Mama held her peace.

Finally, he toppled a dainty figurine to the floor. It smashed on the hearth, its head rolling one way, its body the other. The noise it made was unnaturally loud. Mama winced.

The captain looked mournful. "Now, ain't that just too bad. It would be a terrible shame if I was to lose my temper. Why, there wouldn't be one pretty thing left."

The only sounds were the frozen rain ticking against the windows and the wind blowing around the house, cold and lonely and full of sorrow. My heart rode with James Marshall through the darkness, but my body stayed close to Mama, fearful of what was yet to come.

"If my men catch Marshall," the captain said, "I might leave you enough to get by till spring. But if the villain escapes, I'll see to it you have nothing."

He paused. "Of course, I could find it my heart to be merciful, ma'am. I'm not by nature a cruel man. Indeed, at home in Pittsburgh I'm respected by the best people in town." He paused and flexed his sword blade against his thumb. "Perhaps we could discuss my proposal in private."

Mama's face paled and she backed away.

The captain reached out and took Mama's arm. Pulling her close to him, he whispered, "If you don't want your children harmed, I suggest you come upstairs with me now."

Rachel and I clung to Mama, terrified to let her go. Gently she pried our hands away. In a soft voice, she said, "I think it's best for us all if I listen to what the captain has to say. Please stay here and be still."

"That's very sensible, ma'am," Captain Powell said.

In disbelief, Rachel and I watched Captain Powell follow Mama upstairs. She kept her back straight and her head high.

Rachel began to cry. She would have chased after Mama if I hadn't stopped her.

"Mama said to wait here," I said. It was hard to speak, for my mouth was dry and my tongue felt as if it had swollen to twice its natural size. I wasn't sure I could have climbed those steps, for my knees had melted and I could barely stand.

Upstairs the captain slammed the bedroom door. In the

deadly quiet, we both heard the key turn, locking us out. Never had I felt so useless in my life. If only I were older and braver. If only I had a gun or the gumption to fight for Mama. It seemed I was nothing but a puny weakling, of no more help than Rachel.

◦ 4 ◦

RACHEL AND I WAITED at the foot of the steps, praying to God to keep our mama from harm. We heard nothing from upstairs. Not one sound. Rachel began to cry.

Suddenly, a gunshot shattered the silence.

Rachel screamed. Like me, she must have thought the captain had shot Mama. I wanted to run upstairs, but I still couldn't make myself move.

I heard the bedroom door open and then slam shut. Rachel buried her face in my shirt and clung to me. I shut my eyes to keep from seeing the captain pointing his gun at us.

"Haswell, Rachel," Mama called in a high, unnatural voice.

I opened my eyes and looked up. Mama stood at the top of the stairs. Her face was dead white, her hair tumbled in a tangled mass down her back, and the front of her dress was torn. Worst of all, she was spattered with blood. Face, hair, dress. In one hand was the revolver Papa had given her for protection.

"Mama, you're bleeding," I cried.

"It's his blood, not mine," she whispered. "God forgive me, I've killed him."

Rachel and I ran upstairs. My sister flung her arms

around Mama. "We thought he'd killed you," she sobbed. "We thought you were dead."

Mama paid no mind to Rachel. She went on speaking in that high, trembling voice. "I took the pistol out from under the pillow. I shot him dead."

I started to open the bedroom door to make sure he was truly dead, but Mama stopped me. "Don't look. I shot him in the face."

"What will those men do when they come back?" Rachel whispered. "Will they hang us?"

"Maybe we should hide," I said.

"I killed him," Mama said. "I took the pistol from under the pillow and I, and I—"

"Mama." I shook her gently, hoping to bring her back from wherever she'd gone. "Mama, what should we do now?"

"Thou shalt not kill," Mama murmured. "Thou shalt not—"

Rachel began to cry. "Mama, Mama," she begged. "He was a wicked man, he tried to hurt you."

"You had to kill him, Mama," I said. "You had to!"

But nothing we said had any effect. Mama stood there, the revolver dangling from her hand, and stared about her as if she saw nothing.

I took the revolver from her and stuck it the waistband of my pants. She didn't move or speak. She might as well have been walking in her sleep.

It scared me to see her like that, for she'd been the same when the last baby died. Grieving and mourning, blaming herself for poor little Benjamin's death. Her milk had been bad, she hadn't kept him warm enough, she'd neglected him in some basic way that had made him sicken and die. None of it was true. Doctor Adams told her over and over the baby had come early and was too small to live, but it was at least six months before she stopped crying whenever she thought of him.

Papa said Mama was delicate. She took life hard. In bad times, he'd been there to comfort her, to love her back to life. But Papa had been dead more than a year and Mama was still grieving him. If only I'd had the revolver, if only I'd been the one to shoot the captain. But no, it had to be poor, delicate Mama.

While Rachel hugged Mama and tried to comfort her, I put my mind to work. We had to do something before the soldiers came back. Get rid of the captain's body, clean up the blood, hide his horse. We'd need the horse ourselves if we managed to survive the night.

I squeezed my sister's arm to get her attention. "Stay with Mama, Rachel. I have to hide the horse."

I opened the front door to a blast of wind and sleet. The captain's horse was tied to the porch railing, waiting patiently. He let me lead him across the icy grass and into the woods. No doubt he thought I was a groom come to take him to the barn and feed him, dry his coat, and cover him with a blanket. He wasn't going to be happy when he learned the truth.

I took him down into the gully and tied him to a tree. I didn't want anyone to hear if he whinnied. Which he did loudly. "Hush," I said, stroking his sides and neck. "Hush, now. You're all right here. Safe. I aim to take good care of you."

When I'd managed to calm the horse somewhat, I headed back to the house. The sleet was still falling, pricking my face till my skin stung. I dreaded the task that lay ahead of me. But I was the only one fit to hide the captain's body. Lord, I wished Avery were here. He always knew what to do, and the best way to accomplish it. I cursed him under my breath.

And James Marshall, too. If only he'd chosen some other farm. Why in God's name had he stopped at our door, bringing the devil with him? And now he was free, riding back to Mosby to win more glory, leaving us to deal with the Yankees. Nothing in this world was fair, and that was the truth. It was enough to make me doubt God's goodness. What if Our Lord sat on high like Zeus and watched us suffer? Maybe He sent angels to help those He favored. Maybe the devil sent fiends to help those *he* favored.

At the house I found Rachel and Mama sitting at the kitchen table. Rachel had fixed tea and was trying to get Mama to drink it, but Mama's hand shook so bad she couldn't hold the cup steady. Her face was clean of the captain's blood, but her dress was still soaked with it. I'd never seen Mama kill as much as a mouse or even a spider. She was the sort that caught them as gently as she could and set them outside. Papa used to tease her about her tender heart. He might not have recognized her when she'd opened that bedroom door, holding the revolver in her hand, and told us what she'd done.

"Are you feeling better, Mama?" I asked.

She didn't answer, just sat there clutching the cup, her hair loose, her face blank. I'd seen a woman being hauled off to the county poor farm once. Avery had told me she'd gone crazy—that was why her husband was sending her away. It seemed a hard thing to do, but the woman didn't seem to care where they took her. She'd sat in the wagon, her head down, her eyes as vacant as Mama's were now.

Rachel patted Mama's shoulder and stroked her hair.

"It will be all right, Mama. Haswell's taking care of every-thing."

"Haswell's a boy," Mama whispered. "Avery's no help, either. He's never here when troubles come. We need Papa. He'd know what to do." She turned her face to the window. "When is Burton coming back?"

Rachel and I looked at each other. "But, Mama," Rachel said, "Papa can't come back. He's, he's—don't you remember?"

"Oh, yes." Mama sighed. "The war. He's at the war. I begged and begged Burton not to get involved in all that killing and dying. But he went anyway. Out of duty and honor, he said."

Mama struck the table with her fist. Tea slopped over the rim of her cup. "His duty is here," she said. "To us. Honor and glory—what good are they to anybody but a fool?"

I touched Mama's shoulder lightly. "Drink your tea, Mama. I swear I'll make things right. Just trust me." To tell the truth, I was getting edgy. Those soldiers could come back any minute. Fearful a task as it was, I had to hide the captain's body before they returned.

Mama looked up at me, her eyes sharpening. "You're a good boy, Haswell. Promise me you won't run off to the war. Stay home, read your Bible—" Her voice broke and she began to cry.

I patted her hand. "I promise to stay here and take care of you. I promise, Mama." Turning to Rachel. I said, "Try to calm her."

Leaving them in the kitchen, I walked slowly down the hall and climbed the stairs like an old man, one step at a time, dreading the task before me. At the closed bedroom door, I paused. It wasn't as if I'd never seen a dead person. Folks died all the time. Grandfather Colby, Grandmother and Grandfather Magruder, a great aunt, my baby brother. They'd been laid out properly, their faces peaceful, their hands crossed on their breasts. They'd looked as if they'd been expecting death somehow and were content to go with him.

Since the war began, I'd seen worse deaths—soldiers killed in skirmishes and left where they'd fallen in the woods by the road. Some boys stole the corpses' uniform buttons and searched their pockets. Not me. I hadn't looked at them closely and I'd never touched one. Those soldiers hadn't gone peacefully. They'd been taken unawares, and the sight of their sprawled bodies scared me. They didn't lie there long. Somebody, usually soldiers, fetched them and did the burying.

But this time, it was I, Haswell Colby Magruder, who had to do the fetching and the burying. And I had to do it fast.

I took a deep breath and slowly eased the door open. The kerosene lamp burned low beside the bed, casting long shadows on the wall. The wind tugged at the shutters just enough to make them rap against the house. I could see the captain sprawled on the bed, his face hidden in the shadows. The wind rose and banged the shutters harder. It blew in through the cracks and the kerosene lamp flickered. The shadows wavered and made me think the captain was about to sit up. I backed away, reaching for the revolver, preparing to shoot him again and again until I was sure he was dead.

When he failed to move, I forced myself to walk to the side of the bed. My legs were weak and a vile taste surged up my throat, but I made myself look at the captain. Half his head was blown away. His blood soaked the sheets and quilts and pillows with crimson. His one remaining eye glared at me in fury. If the dead could curse, I was damned for all eternity.

Much as I feared to touch him, I hauled him off the bed. His body hit the wooden floor with a dull thud that shivered my flesh. His arms and legs twitched as if he were coming back to life after all. I jumped back, my heart pounding, and watched him settle down. When I was once again sure he was dead, I wrapped him in a quilt Mama had made, ruined now with blood and gore. I remembered her piecing it together in a pattern she called the Drunkard's Path, working hard all through the warm months so it would be ready for winter's cold nights.

Just as I finished wrapping the captain's body, I heard a small sound. Rachel stood in the doorway, staring at me and the corpse.

"How long have you been standing there?"

"Since that loud noise," she whispered. "I was scared something had happened, that maybe he wasn't dead after all."

"Did you see him?"

Rachel shuddered. "I never saw anything so horrible in my life. All that blood. How did you dare touch him?"

"I had to. We've got to get him out of the house, hide him somewhere. If those soldiers see him . . ."

Rachel looked past me at the bed. "How are you going to clean that mess up?"

"With water and a scrub brush, I reckon."

"That will take a long time," Rachel said. "What if the soldiers come back before you're done?"

I looked down at the body and then at the bloody bed.

The soldiers had been gone for about thirty minutes. They were sure to be back soon, cold and angry and empty-handed.

"You could leave him in here and lock the door," Rachel suggested.

Before I left the room, I scooped up the bullets Papa had kept in the top dresser drawer and dropped them into my pocket. Though I hoped I wouldn't need them, it was smart to be prepared for calamity.

Although I disliked the idea of agreeing with a seven-year-old girl, Rachel's idea made sense. "We could tell his men he left to join them," I said.

"And they must have missed him in the dark," Rachel added. "So they should go find him right away."

Turning our backs on the captain's body, we locked the door, and ran downstairs to the kitchen.

Mama was still at the table, the empty teacup clutched in her hands, as if she was trying to warm them. I sat down opposite her and took the cup from her. Holding her hands, I told her I'd hidden the captain's horse and left his body in the bedroom. "When the soldiers come back, we'll tell them the captain rode after them. They must have missed him in the dark."

"And he said for them to follow him at once," Rachel put in.

"I killed him," Mama whispered, "I killed him."

"No, don't say that!" I cried. "We can't let on anything's wrong."

I turned to Rachel. "Help her fix her hair."

While Rachel fetched the comb and hairpins, I draped a shawl over Mama's shoulders to hide the tear in her dress and the blood staining the front. "You have to act as if nothing happened."

Mama turned to me, tears running down her face, "But, Haswell," she sobbed. "I killed him. There was blood everywhere. Oh, God, forgive me."

"Mama, please." I held her hands so tight I could feel her bones. "Please don't carry on like this. You did what you had to do. The Lord knows that."

Mama lowered her head and plucked at her skirt. "His blood is soaking through my dress. I feel it on my skin."

It wouldn't do. Mama would tell those soldiers what she'd done. They'd kill us all then. Even if Mama kept quiet, they might take her upstairs the way the captain had. And then they'd most likely kill us. I'd heard rumors of such things happening to women left alone on farms. Deserters from both sides, soldiers bent on vengeance— it didn't matter whether they were from the North or the South sometimes. Depended on their nature. The last time Papa had come home, he'd said war lets out the beast in men. Now I knew what he'd meant.

I got Mama to her feet and told Rachel to fetch our coats and all the blankets she could carry.

"Why?" she asked.

"Because we're going to hide in the gully down in the woods. We don't dare stay here and wait for those men to come back."

Rachel looked at me as if I'd lost my wits. "But, Haswell, it's cold and it's sleeting. And it's dark."

I grabbed her shoulders and peered into her eyes. "We can't trust Mama not to tell those Yankees exactly what she did. And then what do you think they'll do to us?"

There must have been something in my voice that scared her, for she scurried away and came back as fast as she could, loaded down with coats and blankets. We bundled Mama up as best we could and struggled to get her out the door.

"No," she cried. "I must stay here and be punished for what I did."

Ignoring her cries, Rachel and I managed to force her through the door.

The wind blasted us with sleet. Slipping and sliding on the icy ground, we made our way across the yard. Mama's lamentations mingled with the sound of the wind. At any moment I expected to see the Yankees riding toward us, their guns aimed at our heads.

· 5 ·

ONCE WE WERE AMONGST the trees, we had some shelter from the wind, but the ground was so icy we could scarcely stay on our feet. I headed toward the gully where I'd hidden the captain's horse. He stood where I'd left him, enduring the sleet. When he saw me, he raised his head and whinnied. I wished I'd thought to bring a handful of oats for him. But at the moment, Rachel and Mama were my concern. Passing the horse by, I led the two of them under a rock overhang.

"I'm cold," Rachel whispered. Her teeth were chattering, and I could feel her shaking on one side of me and Mama on the other. Mama was still muttering about blood and hellfire.

"We're all cold, Rachel," I said. "Just be still and listen for those men."

Whimpering to herself, Rachel snuggled into Mama's side like a newborn kitten trying to warm itself. Mama put her arm around Rachel, but it was just a gesture. She didn't seem concerned about either Rachel or me. Or herself. Whether we survived the night or not made no difference to her.

For a while all we heard was the wind lashing the trees and the sleet pattering on the ground. Then my ears caught the sound of voices. I'd been certain they'd be coming from the other direction, but they were only a few feet away, riding along a trail at the top of the gully.

I hugged Mama and Rachel, praying they'd keep quiet. "I'll be right back," I whispered. "Stay here and don't make a sound."

Thinking the sound of the storm would cover any noise I made, I crept up to the edge of the gully and watched the men ride toward me.

"We must be almost there," Anderson said.

"Won't the captain be pleased when he sees what we got?" The man riding close behind laughed.

"He ain't so sassy now." The Yankee glanced at the black horse he was leading. A body lay across its back. It was James Marshall, clearly dead. I reached for Papa's revolver, thinking I'd murder the devils, but in the dark, with the trees around, I had no hope of killing all three. I'd end up giving Mama and Rachel's hiding place away. Filled with hatred, I crouched behind a rock and watched the Yankees file past.

"Powell better show us some gratitude," Anderson said. "He's been snug and warm while we been out here freezing our asses off."

"Pray them Rebs ain't Methodists or Baptists. I could use a whiskey long 'bout now."

"How about you, Hicks? Some fire in your belly might give you some grit."

Hicks didn't say anything. He rode his horse in a dispirited way, his head hanging down as if he were close to sleeping.

The men disappeared into the darkness. Long after they were out of sight, I could hear them laughing and cursing.

I slid back down the hill, my heart heavy with grief for

James Marshall. It shamed me to think I'd blamed our troubles on him and now he was dead. Mama had cured him only for him to die.

"Are they gone?" Rachel asked in a scared little voice.

"Yes."

"Did they catch James Marshall?"

I put my arm around her. "I'm afraid they did."

"Is he dead?"

I hugged her closer. "Yes."

Rachel began to cry. Mama prayed to herself, keeping her voice low. The wind blew, and the sleet fell. The rock protected us from the worst of it, but we were mighty cold and wet. I wished I could build a fire, but I was scared the men would see it. We had no choice but to hunker down and stay put.

It wasn't long till we heard the men calling for the captain. We were too far away to make out what else they said. They quieted down after a while. The silence was worse than the yelling, for it most likely meant they were planning vengeance. We'd sheltered a Ranger, and we were bound to pay a penalty for it. Worse yet, we'd killed a Union officer. If they found the captain's body, we were surely doomed.

Half an hour or so passed. My toes were numb from the cold, and my fingers ached so bad I could barely hold the revolver. Every now and then I heard sounds from the house. Breaking glass, furniture splintering, loud laughter, swearing, even a few gunshots. Most likely the Yankees had found Papa's liquor.

Time passed. No one came roaring outside, shouting to us murdering rebels to surrender. The Yankees stayed in the house, getting drunker and drunker. They sang barroom songs, they cursed, they shouted insults at Hicks. But they didn't come searching for us.

After a while, Rachel nudged me, waking me from a light sleep. "Look, Haswell, is that the sun coming up already?"

I turned where she pointed, not to the east but to the north, where no sun ever rose. The devils had set fire to the house or the barn, maybe both. I heard more gunshots, more laughter.

"But how can it be the sun?" Rachel went on. "It's still darkest night."

Mama wept. Like me, she knew what that light in the sky meant.

"It's our house," Rachel cried. "They're burning it!" She leapt to her feet and tried to climb up the muddy side of the gully. "My doll," she sobbed. "I left Sophia in her cradle."

I grabbed my sister and pulled her back under the rock. She struggled and kicked and bit, all the while crying for her doll.

"You want the Yankees to burn you up, too?" I hissed in her ear.

"They wouldn't harm a girl!" Rachel cried.

"Oh, yes, they would," I said. "We have to stay hidden."

Rachel stopped struggling, but she kept on sobbing for Sophia.

The night passed slowly. The fire died down. So did the noise. But I was scared to go see if the soldiers were gone. They could be sleeping or lying in wait for us to appear.

So we stayed where we were, huddled as close to one another as we could get, and waited for dawn. I don't think any of us got any real sleep. I might have shut my eyes a few times, but the cold always woke me up. That and Mama's coughing.

By the time the sky turned gray in the east, I ached like an old man. Shaking off my damp blanket, I got to my feet as quietly as I could. Mama was awake, her eyes fixed on me.

"What are we going to do, Haswell?" she asked fearfully.

Her question took me by surprise, for I was used to her telling me what to do, not me telling her. I thought a second. "Why, I suppose I should sneak closer and see what they've done."

"You know the house is gone," Mama said slowly. "And the barn, too, most likely." There was no emotion in her voice. She spoke as dully as if she were telling me about a stranger's misfortune, not her own. "It's the Lord's way of punishing me for what I did. Killing is against His commandments."

I opened my mouth to try once more to convince her she had done nothing to displease the Lord, but Rachel chose that moment to pop up from her blankets, her hair as frowzy as a rag doll's. "If you go up to the house, find Sophia and bring her to me. Even if she's all burned up. And food. Get us something to eat. I'm perishing of cold and hunger."

I leaned down and whispered, "Stay close to Mama, Rachel, but don't pester her. She's not feeling well."

I left the two of them huddled under the blankets and crept out of the gully as quietly as I could. The captain's horse swung his head toward me hopefully, but I had nothing for him.

The storm had passed and the air was gray with a fog so dense it might have been a cloud sunk down to earth.

At the edge of the trees, I looked in the direction of the house. Despite the fog, I should have been able to see something. I smelled smoke and burning but heard and saw nothing.

Taking advantage of the fog, I crept across the yard, moving like a ghost myself. No sign of the Yankees or their horses. And no sign of the house except a few blackened timbers and charred wood. The chimney rose as straight and true as Grandpa Magruder had built it. The smell of smoke and burning hung heavy in the air. The stench stung tears from my eyes.

The barn was gone, too, along with our cow. The only thing the Yankees had left behind was James Marshall.

Even though he was dead already, they'd hanged him from the maple in the yard. He was a fearsome sight, stiff and swinging slowly in the morning wind. The rope creaked every time his body turned. I noticed they'd taken his greatcoat and his fine boots.

It wouldn't do for Mama and Rachel to see such a cruel sight. I climbed up into the maple and slowly sawed the rope through with my hunting knife. James Marshall hit the icy ground and lay stiff and still.

I climbed down and bent over him. From the look of his bloody shirt, he'd been shot more than once. Not in the back but in the front, which meant he'd been facing those Yankees when he took the bullets.

A note pinned to his shirt said, "This is what happens to Mosby's Bushwhackers and them that shelter them." It was signed, "Capt. Powell's men."

A flock of crows winged their way across the sky and settled in the maple's branches. They cawed and scolded and jostled one another. It was clear they meant to make a meal of James Marshall as soon as I turned my back.

As gently as I could, I dragged his body to the spring-house and laid him out on the stone floor. All was still except for the stream that cooled our milk. It gurgled through its channel, but not one milk jug blocked its path. The Yankees hadn't missed a thing. They meant us to starve or freeze.

"I'm sorry to see you in this state," I whispered to James Marshall. "I was certain you'd get away from those Yankees."

I smoothed his dark hair and set stones on his eyelids to keep them closed. I should have used pennies, but I didn't have any. I said some prayers for James Marshall's soul, which I hoped was resting over Jordan in the shade of the trees. He was a good man and he'd died a good death. But I mourned him with all my soul.

"Later on I'll do my best to bury you proper," I said, "but you're safe here for now."

I rose slowly to my feet and wiped my eyes. Though I hated to do it, I left him there and closed the springhouse door tight. No crow, fox, or wild dog would get James Marshall.

With that sad task taken care of, I went back to the remains of the house and climbed down into the root cellar. Lucky for us, the Yankees hadn't taken time to look or they would have stolen Mama's preserves, as well as the fruit and vegetables she kept there. I filled my pockets with apples and made my way back to the gully.

Mama and Rachel greeted me as if I'd been gone a week or more. While we munched apples, I told them the house and barn were both burned to the ground.

"What about my doll?" Rachel asked. "Did you find Sophia?"

"The house is still smoldering, Rachel. It's not safe to go inside."

Her face collapsed and she started crying. "I hate those Yankees; I wish you'd killed them all."

"Now, Rachel," I began, but she cut me off.

"Why couldn't you have let James Marshall go on by, like Mama told you? If he hadn't come along—"

"Rachel, Rachel," Mama pulled her close. "Don't say such things. James Marshall was a fine young man. Suppose our Avery was sick and wounded? Would you want people to turn him away because they were scared of the Yankees?"

Rachel clung to Mama and wept. It was clear that Mama barely had the strength to comfort the child, but she did her best. At least she was acting more like herself. It must have been the first time since she'd killed the captain that Mama hadn't spoken of her guilt. Maybe she was getting over it.

"Come on," I said. "Let's go back to the house. We can shelter in the root cellar, build a fire, dry ourselves out."

Rachel let go of Mama and scrambled up the gully, her spirits already rising at the thought of a warm fire. I followed more slowly, helping Mama, who seemed to have lost her strength entirely. She leaned on me as if she were Grandma Colby's age, breathing hard and coughing deep in her chest. Her body felt warm, and her hand heated mine.

By the time we reached the house, I was practically carrying Mama. She paused and looked at the ruins, still smoking in the cold damp air, and sighed. "When your papa comes home, he'll have a sight of work to do," was all she said.

It seemed Mama was slipping away from us again.

Surely her fever was affecting her mind. I'd had spells myself when I was sick, seeing things that weren't there, hearing voices in the dead of the night, crying out nonsense.

Rachel tugged at Mama's hand. "But, Mama," she began, "Papa—"

I squeezed Rachel's shoulder hard. "Shh," I whispered. "Let Mama think what she wants. She's not herself right now. Fever does that to a person."

Rachel bit her lip and edged away from Mama and me. She looked frightened. I guessed she was too young to understand what was happening. "I'm going to look for my doll," she announced loudly.

"Don't go in the house," I said. "That fire's still smoldering."

Rachel turned and ran off toward the front of the house. I was inclined to go after her, but Mama grabbed my arm. "What did they do with James Marshall, Haswell?"

"They left his body here. I put him in the springhouse."

She nodded. "He'll be safe there till Burton comes home and we can bury him proper."

Ignoring her remark, I eased Mama down the stone steps to the root cellar. The earth smelled cold and moldy, but I figured a fire would drive off the damp. If I could warm Mama, get some food into her, talk sense to her, she might recover her wits.

I laid a blanket on the ground for Mama to lie on and piled the others on top of her. Just as I was getting a fire going, I saw Rachel at the top of the steps.

"Haswell, Mama, look!" She held up her doll. "I found Sophia. She was lying in the yard. And she's not even hurt!"

Rachel ran down the steps. "Those Yankees must have

meant to kidnap her." She hugged the doll tight. "But she escaped."

"Smart Sophia," I said.

After Mama and Rachel settled down, I got a fire going to warm them. Then I went off to fetch the captain's horse. I had plans for that animal. As soon as she was strong enough, I meant to put Mama on his back and take her and Rachel to Grandma Colby's farm. It wasn't more than twenty miles down the Winchester Road, way too far for Mama to walk but easy enough for Rachel and me. We'd be safe with Mama's Mama. Old and cranky as she was, Grandma Colby would cure Mama.

I was relieved to find the horse where I'd left him, still tied to the tree. Despite his Yankee breeding, he was a handsome chestnut with a black tail and mane, almost as splendid as James Marshall's horse, broad across the shoulders and strong-legged, built for riding hard.

Cautiously I held an apple out. He nickered and rolled his eyes, showing the whites. At the same time he bared his big yellow teeth and pawed the ground with his front hoof. But he took the apple without biting me. I guessed he was too hungry to be particular about taking food from a Rebel.

While he ate it, I talked to him, pitching my voice soft and low. "You've got good lines," I told him. "Nice mane and tail, too. A little brushing will shine your coat up real pretty."

He nickered again, but he didn't look so mean. "Maybe you're just tired of being tied to a tree. Most likely you're used to better quarters."

He watched me come closer. When I reached for the reins, he started pawing the ground again and looking skittish.

"Don't fret yourself," I whispered. "The captain's gone, and I'm going to take good care of you. I've always wanted a horse like you."

Though it took all my courage, I moved slowly nearer and untied the reins. "Stay," I said, "stay."

The horse shivered, but he obeyed. Holding the reins firmly, I started walking back to the house. The horse followed without making a fuss. Despite his evil ways toward people, the captain had trained the animal well.

One corner of the stable had survived the fire, so I tied the horse there and found hay for him. I also fetched him a pail of water, which meant going to the springhouse. James Marshall lay where I'd left him, as still as ever, his eyes shut, his face sunken, his skin bluish white. Most of the dead I'd seen looked peaceful, but not James Marshall. His face was twisted in pain and anger.

A terrible sadness fell upon me, shutting out everything but the dead man. Somewhere folks—his father and his mother, his sweetheart, his sister—waited for him to come home, worried about him, missed him. They had no way of knowing they'd never see him again, never hear his voice.

These thoughts put me in mind of Avery. What if he were dead and no one had told us yet? I shook my head. Surely I'd feel his passing. He'd come to me in a dream or send me a vision. If my brother had joined Papa across the River Jordan, I'd know.

To keep from fretting, I took the water to the horse. "Since I have no idea what the captain named you, I'm calling you Ranger." I stroked his muzzle, pleased with the name, for I knew it was one the captain would despise. "Ranger," I repeated, "Ranger. Like one of Mosby's company. You think you can remember that, Ranger?"

Ranger bent his head over the bucket and drank. I

stayed with him a while, telling him about myself and my family and how he was now our horse. I was hoping he'd get used to my smell and the sound of my voice.

After a time, I heard Rachel calling me. Her voice filled me with alarm, for it rang with urgency and fear. Leaving Ranger, I ran toward the house as fast as I could go.

ᐧ 6 ᐧ

"HASWELL!" RACHEL HURRIED to meet me. "Where have you been? Mama's gone down to the river to wash. I couldn't stop her!" She pulled at me, frantic with fear. "I said it's too cold, but she told me to leave her be, she had to wash the blood away."

I ran toward the river, with Rachel leading the way. We found Mama up to her neck in the water. Her long hair floated on the surface, and her dress billowed around her. I plunged in and grabbed her hands, shocked breathless by icy-cold water.

Mama looked at me as if I were a stranger. "Is the blood gone? Is it washed away?" she asked.

"Come out of the water, Mama," I gasped. "You'll freeze to death."

"But is the blood gone?"

"Yes," I said. "Yes, it's gone."

"Are you certain?" She peered at me. "The Lord won't allow me into heaven with blood on my hands. I broke a commandment. I killed a man."

I kept pulling her toward shore. The current ran swift. I lost my footing a couple of times and fell, but I kept hold of Mama. Rachel stood on the bank, shivering and crying.

"Sweet Jesus," Mama prayed, "forgive me. Please forgive me."

Somehow I got her to the edge of the river. With Rachel pulling from above and me pushing from below, we got her up the muddy bank. Out of the water, the cold air hit me like a gust of wind from the North Pole.

"Mama, Mama," Rachel wept.

Mama pushed her aside and staggered on through the trees. Rachel ran beside her. "Mama, what's wrong? Be yourself, please, Mama, be yourself!"

But Mama didn't so much as look at Rachel. She was too deep in prayer to notice where she was or what she was doing. Somehow, we steered her to the root cellar. The fire had died down with no one to tend it. I got it going again and turned to Rachel.

"Get Mama out of those wet clothes and wrap her in a blanket. I'll fetch more wood."

For once, Rachel did as I told her. By the time I came back with logs from the woodpile, Mama was sitting by the fire, draped in blankets but shivering. Her long brown hair waved over her shoulders like a young girl's, but the grief in her face was an old woman's.

I stripped in a corner and wrapped up in my blanket. Rachel had hung Mama's clothing near the fire, and I put mine beside them. I was still cold, but at least I was dry.

Mama looked at me. "Haswell." She touched my cheek. "Why is it so easy to kill a man? In an instant he was gone."

While I tried to think of an answer, she went on talking, more to herself than me. "I only meant to stop him. Not kill him."

"Mama, it was the same as killing in war. The good Lord understands such acts."

Rachel put her arms around Mama. "He was a wicked man, and he's in hell right now."

"No," Mama whispered, "no, I didn't mean to send him there. I should have let him repent, I should have given him time to save his soul."

"Please stop fretting, Mama," I begged. "You did what you had to, that's all."

"But the trigger," Mama went on as if I hadn't spoken. "I just gave it a squeeze and it—" She broke off and began crying. "Oh, Haswell, I never dreamed I could kill a man."

I don't know how long Rachel and I tried to comfort Mama. Nothing we said reached her. It was like speaking to a tree or a stone. Finally, she fell into a troubled sleep.

Rachel found three good-sized potatoes and put them in the fire to bake. "I'll fetch a bucket of water from the springhouse," she said.

"No." I jumped to my feet, stumbling over the blanket. "I'll get it."

Rachel gave me a surprised look. "Fetching water is my chore."

"James Marshall is there," I said.

"I thought he was dead."

"He is."

Rachel's face crumpled. "I didn't want him to die. He made us so happy that night. Remember the singing? And Mama playing the organ?" Tears ran down her face, leaving streaks on her dirty cheeks. "I want to say good-bye to him, Haswell. And pray for him."

"We can't leave Mama," I said.

"You stay with her," Rachel said. "I'll go."

"All by yourself?"

"I'll take Sophia."

I watched her run off toward the springhouse, lugging the doll. It was her wish. She was far too obstinate to listen to anything I might say about the dead and their terrible silence.

I squatted down beside Mama and felt her forehead. As I'd feared, her skin was still burning-hot to the touch. A fit of coughing woke her and she looked at me.

"Haswell," she murmured. "I was dreaming of Burton. He came riding out of the mist and called my name." She stopped to cough, her gaze unfocused as if she were still seeing Papa. "I ran to him and it was springtime. We were young. Birds sang the sweetest songs. It was like heaven."

I had to lean close to hear her, for her voice was low and hoarse and she couldn't speak easily.

"That was a wonderful dream," I said. Her fever-bright eyes reminded me of James Marshall on his first night with us. Mama had nursed him through his illness. But how was I to nurse her?

"Yes, it was." Mama smiled. "I love your papa so much." Her smile faded and the troubled look returned. "But he shouldn't have gone off to war."

"He had to go, Mama. You know that."

She shook her head and frowned. "War means killing, and killing's wrong. It's wrong, Haswell."

I patted her hand and she began coughing again, harder this time, as if she'd never stop. "Where's Rachel gone to?" she asked when she could.

"To the springhouse, for water."

Mama nodded. "I'm so cold," she whispered.

"When Rachel comes with the water, I'll brew sassafras tea," I told Mama. But she was already asleep.

Just as I was thinking I'd have to go find Rachel, she appeared at the top of the steps, holding Sophia.

"Where's the water?" I asked.

She came down the steps and huddled beside me. "Why did he have to die?"

"Oh, Rachel." It seemed everyone asked me questions I couldn't answer.

"He looked so sad," she went on. "It fair broke my heart." The tears started then, and I hugged her tight. She was a skinny little thing, bony in my arms and shivering as if she'd never be warm again.

We sat together till she stopped crying. Then I put on my damp clothes and went to get the water. I glanced at James Marshall. He lay as still as before. If only he'd open his eyes and sit up and not be dead after all. But that only happened in dreams. He wasn't ever going to be alive again.

I carried a pail of water back to the root cellar, and Rachel brewed sassafras tea. We woke Mama when it was ready and got her to drink some, but she wouldn't eat more than a mouthful of the potato.

"I'm not hungry," she said. "You eat it."

Since we couldn't persuade her differently, Rachel and I divided Mama's potato between us. Though I wished Mama had eaten it herself, I didn't want to waste food.

◇

The day passed slowly. Mama slept, coughed, woke, slept again. In a wakeful spell she told Rachel how to make soup with the carrots, parsnips, turnips, onions, and potatoes she'd stored in the root cellar.

"It would taste better if we had salt and a good beef bone," Mama said, "but we'll have to make do with what we have." She smiled at Rachel and patted her hand.

For a moment Mama seemed like her old self, and I let myself hope she was getting better. I listened to her give Rachel a few tips about making biscuits and peach cobblers, baking bread and deep-dish apple pies. Unfortunately, we had no flour, and so my stomach growled in vain for the delicacies Mama used to make for us.

Gradually her speech slowed and her voice dropped and she was asleep again, waking herself now and then with coughing spells.

"Is there any more of that medicine Mama brewed for James Marshall?" Rachel asked. "It might help her."

I shook my head. "I reckon everything burned up in the fire."

"I should have listened when Mama tried to teach me about herbs." Rachel sat with her knees drawn up tight and rested her chin on them. Her voice dropped to a whisper. "But I couldn't bear the way those things smelled. I always ran off. I knew how to make myself scarce, Mama said."

She raised her head and looked at me. "Why didn't I learn about remedies and cures and such? Grandma Colby's right about me. I'm a lazy, sinful girl."

I patted her shoulder. "Don't carry on so, Rachel. How could you know something like this would happen?"

"If Mama dies, it'll be all my fault."

"Mama won't die!" This time I shouted in her face and shook her. I wasn't about to let my sister say a frightful thing like that. It didn't bear thinking about, let alone saying out loud.

Rachel squirmed away from me and put some distance between us. "But what if she does, Haswell? What will happen to us? Where will we go? Who will shelter us?"

Rachel's voice rose so high she woke Mama. She reached out and grabbed my wrist with her hot hand.

"Rachel's right to worry," Mama whispered. "If I die, promise you'll go to your Grandma Colby. But be careful.

War is everywhere these days. War and killing." She broke off and started another coughing fit.

"We'll all go to Grandma Colby's," I told her. "I'll put you on the captain's horse, and Rachel and I will walk alongside of you. You'll look like a queen."

Mama shook her head, coughing too hard to speak.

"Here, Mama." Rachel held out another cup of sassafras tea. "Drink this."

Mama's hands shook so badly she couldn't hold the cup, so Rachel carefully spooned it into her mouth. After a few sips, Mama turned her head away. "Enough, Rachel, enough." Gazing past us to the square of sky outside the root cellar door, she smiled. "Your papa's coming," she whispered. "Everything will be all right when he gets here."

Mama's head fell back and her eyes closed. Once again she slept. Rachel and I sat beside her and fed the fire to keep her warm. The sun slid down the sky, turning the clouds scarlet and purple, as if all heaven was afire. A preacher might have claimed it was the end of the world at last, but the colors soon faded to dull grays and lavender, and it was an ordinary night after all.

The next time Mama woke, Rachel and I tried to feed her the soup, but she turned her head away. We sat by her and ate our portions.

"Is it all right?" Rachel asked me.

"What? The soup?"

She nodded, her eyes on mine. "Is it as good as Mama's?"

I took another big swallow and smiled. "Why, it's delicious, Rachel. You're a very good cook."

Rachel sighed happily and went on eating. Though I never, ever would have told her so, the soup was flat and watery compared to Mama's, but that might have been because she'd had no salt or beef bone to put in the pot. I ate every bit, swallowing with zest, doing my best to make my sister feel good about something.

I went out a few times to fetch wood to keep the fire going. I also fed and watered Ranger, which meant another trip to the springhouse. James Marshall was as quiet as ever, keeping his thoughts to himself the way the dead do. I gazed at him a long while, pondering the mystery of life and death, of heaven and hell, but I can't say I came up with any new notions about these matters. The world just seemed to roll along while we got born and lived and died. Just a little while ago, James Marshall was alive, with no idea his life was almost over. It could be the same with me. With all of us. Alive now . . . dead tomorrow.

I folded my arms tightly across my chest, feeling the living warmth of my own body. Even though I was looking straight at a dead man, I couldn't believe someday I'd be cold and still like James Marshall. How could I, Haswell Colby Magruder, die? How could the world go on without me?

Slowly I reached out and touched James Marshall's face. His skin was as cold as stone and just as hard. It no longer had the feel of human flesh.

I picked up the pail of water and went out, pulling the door shut tight. As I crossed the yard, the moon sailed out from behind the clouds. I watched it race across a patch of dark sky and duck behind another cloud, as if it were running from pursuers.

·7·

IN THE ROOT CELLAR Rachel knelt beside Mama. The firelight lit the two of them like figures in a painting.

Rachel looked up at me. "I coaxed her to drink more tea, but most of it just ran out of her mouth."

I dropped down beside Rachel and took Mama's hand in mine. Her skin near burned me. "Won't you please drink something, Mama?"

She shook her head and coughed. "I told you, your papa's on his way. Don't you hear his horse?"

I listened hard, fearing it could be someone else—one of Captain Powell's men returning to look for us, maybe, or a marauder who'd seen our fire. A fox barked a long way off. The wind sprang up and the tree limbs rattled like dry bones. But even when I went to the cellar door and looked out, I neither saw nor heard a horse.

I sat back down and took hold of Mama's hand again. She murmured Papa's name, and I hoped she was dreaming that nice dream about her and Papa walking in the green woods. Rachel leaned against me, clutching Sophia, and slept like a baby. Every now and then she twitched and squirmed, but nothing woke her. I reckoned she was worn out from all that had happened to us.

At some point Mama began to sing in a voice so low I

had to lean close to hear. "Down in the valley, the valley so low," she sang.

It was her favorite song, the one she lulled Avery and Rachel and me to sleep with when we were little children scared of the dark. I joined in, keeping my voice as low as hers.

"Hear the wind blow, dear, hear the wind blow," we sang. "Down in the valley, hear the wind blow."

Slowly her voice faded and she looked at me and smiled. "Those were good times back then, Haswell. All of us together. Safe. No war. The Valley was so green, so lovely. And we were happy, weren't we?" She closed her eyes again and slept, her hand holding mine tight.

Although I meant to watch Mama all night, I must have fallen asleep, for the next thing I knew the gray light of dawn was creeping down the cellar steps and spreading across the floor like spoiled milk. Rachel had toppled over on her side, sucking her thumb in her sleep. Sophia sprawled beside her, her arms outspread, her china face expressionless.

I looked at Mama, hoping the fever had gone down in the night, but when I reached over and touched her forehead, she felt as hot as ever. She opened her eyes and smiled. "It's Papa," she whispered.

She sounded so sure I looked at the cellar door, expecting to see Papa standing there, not dead after all, ready to make everything right again. But all I saw was the blank gray sky. The flash of hope faded, and I turned back to Mama.

I didn't need to touch her again to know that she was gone. "No." I grabbed Mama's hands. "Come back, Mama, don't leave us!"

Rachel sat up, startled out of her sleep. "Haswell, what's wrong?"

"It's Mama," I wept. "She's—"

Rachel flung herself on Mama, sobbing loud enough to wake her. But Mama was beyond hearing. She neither spoke nor breathed nor moved.

I don't know how long the two of us crouched beside Mama, mourning her passing. At one point Rachel fell asleep, leaving me to sit alone and wonder what to do next. Grandma Colby's house was half a day's ride from our place. If we set out by noon, we'd get there before dark. But how could we leave Mama behind?

By the time Rachel woke up, I'd decided what to do.

My sister looked at Mama and started crying again. "Oh, Haswell," she sobbed, "I was hoping it was just a bad dream."

I stroked her hair. Rachel had never looked so pitiful. Mama had kept her neat and clean, her dresses fresh, her hair combed. Now she looked like the orphan she was, her dress torn and dirty, her face and hands grimy, her unbraided hair a tangled mop.

"What are we going to do?" she asked. "What will become of us?"

"We have to go to Grandma Colby's, like Mama said."

"And leave Mama here?" Rachel stared at me, her face pale under the soot and dirt.

"We'll carry her to the springhouse. She'll be safe there."

Rachel thought about my idea and sighed a deep sigh.

"We can't stay here," I said softly.

Slowly Rachel nodded her head. "But what if Avery comes home? He won't know where Mama is. Or us, either."

"When we get to Grandma Colby's, I'll write him a letter. Or maybe I'll go find him myself and bring him home. Where he ought to be. We need him." Once again my anger grew. What did the army want with a boy like Avery? He should have stayed with us. He should have helped us. He should be here right now telling me what to do.

"You can't go off looking for Avery," Rachel said. "I need you." She started crying again. I put my arms around her and she clung to me, her head pressed against my chest.

Though I said nothing more to my sister, I decided then and there to leave Rachel with Grandma Colby and set out to find Avery. The biggest problem would be getting from here to Petersburg. It was a long way, almost two hundred miles, even farther than Richmond. I'd been to the capital many times to see Papa's relatives. Once I got near the city, I'd keep going south, following signposts to Petersburg. I had a good horse to ride and I was sure I could do it.

Gently I freed myself from my sister's arms. "Help me wrap Mama in her blanket, Rachel."

"We should wash her first," Rachel said softly. "And comb her hair. That's what Mama did when Grandma Magruder died."

Rachel tore off part of her slip and dipped it in the bucket of water I'd brought from the springhouse. Carefully she washed the soot and dirt from Mama's face and did her best to tidy her hair. By the time she was done, Mama looked more like herself. But her face was sad.

I hoped someday I'd remember Mama's smile and her laugh, the bedtime stories she told and the songs she sang. But at that moment I couldn't picture her any way but the way she was now.

Without saying a word to each other, Rachel and I wrapped Mama in the blanket. Somehow we got her up the steps and across the yard. Gently we laid her on the stone floor next to James Marshall. The cold had kept him well. I hoped it wouldn't warm up till Grandma Colby sent someone to bury the two of them properly.

Rachel and I knelt together. When we'd said all the prayers we knew, we kissed Mama and James Marshall good-bye and left the springhouse. After I shut the wooden door tight, Rachel helped me gather stones to heap in front of it to make certain Mama and James Marshall would be safe.

While Rachel watched, I used my pocket knife to carve Mama's and James Marshall's names, followed by "Rest in Piece," on a charred board from the house. I wanted anyone who passed this way to know the springhouse was now a tomb, not a place to seek drinking water. I wished I had flowers or something pretty to place there, but all I saw was patches of snow and ice, gray and ugly under the cloudy winter sky, bare trees and bushes, and what was left of our house.

"We've got nothing now," Rachel said in low voice. "Nothing." She pawed at her runny nose with the back of one hand and clutched Sophia to her chest with the other. "We're orphans, Haswell."

"There's still Avery," I said. "When he comes home, he'll take care of us."

"Avery's our brother, not our parents. Besides, he's an orphan, too." Rachel sniffed and turned away to study the marker I'd made. "You spelled 'peace' wrong," she said.

"I did not. I know how to spell just as well as you do."

"You wrote the wrong word, then. It should be *p-e-a-c-e*

and you wrote *p-i-e-c-e*." With that, she started crying as if she never meant to stop.

I stood beside her, feeling helpless. I knew it wasn't my ignorance that made her cry, but I didn't have any idea what to do or say to comfort her. Finally, I touched her shoulder. "We'd best be going," I said as gently as I could. "I'd like to get to Grandma Colby's house before dark."

Rachel flung her arms around me, letting the doll clatter to the icy ground. "Oh, Haswell," she cried, "I don't want to leave Mama. What if she's not dead? What if she wakes up beside James Marshall in the dark and she can't shove the stones away and we're gone and there's no one to help her?"

"Rachel, Rachel." I held her tight. "Mama's not going to wake up anymore than James Marshall is."

She pulled back and gazed at me. "Are you certain?"

I nodded.

"Can we wait here a while and make sure?"

I looked at the sky. Even though it was covered with thick gray clouds, I could see the sun like a pale spot rising up toward the meridian. I hated to delay. The roads were bad enough in the daytime with soldiers hunting one another in the woods and fields, but at least you could see them coming. After dark, there was no telling what lurked in the bushes or behind the trees.

"Please?" Rachel tugged at my arm to get my attention.

I sighed. "Well, just for a few minutes."

We sat down side by side in front of the pile of stones.

"Should I make another marker with the right 'peace' on it?" I asked Rachel.

"No," she said softly. "People will know what you meant."

I stood up. My rear end was cold right through my trousers from sitting on the ground. "We have to leave, Rachel. While I saddle Ranger, go to the root cellar and gather all the food you can find."

She scowled as if she were about to argue, but she thought better of it. Getting slowly to her feet, she trudged across the muddy yard toward the ruins of our house.

"Bring the blankets, too." I called after her.

Rachel stopped and stared at me. "What on earth for? Grandma Colby has plenty of blankets."

"We can't be certain of anything these days." I didn't want to worry her, but it was the truth.

I went to what was left of the stable and fetched Captain Powell's fine leather saddle from the hitching rail. The big horse sniffed at the saddle, but he stood still while I threw it over his back and adjusted the girth. Every now and then he pawed the ground in an agitated way and rolled his eyes at me. I kept talking the whole time, soothing him with my voice, hoping he'd soon grow accustomed to me.

While Ranger watched, I dumped what was left of the oats into the saddlebags. "See? I'll take good care of you," I whispered. "You'll never have to go into battle again. And I'll never use this." I showed him Captain Powell's whip and he shied away. While he watched, I broke the damnable thing over my knee and tossed the pieces aside.

I stroked his side and told him he was a fine horse. To my relief, he let me lead him out of the barn. He had a graceful walk, and his neck curved in a way that showed his breeding. Yankee-born or not, Ranger was without a doubt a noble steed.

After I boosted Rachel into the saddle, I wrapped her in a blanket and mounted the horse in front of her. She wrapped her arms around my waist, and I felt the doll's china face press into my back One touch of my heels against his sides and Ranger was ready to go.

I looked back once at the ruins of our house. Somewhere in those ashes was the body of Captain Powell. His little daughter would never see him come riding home. Most likely no one would know what had happened to the man. Well, he wasn't the first soldier lost. Nor would he be the last.

Then I turned my face toward the road and left my home behind.

◦ 8 ◦

AT THE END OF OUR LANE, I turned Ranger toward
Grandma Colby's farm. Snow and ice lingered in gray lacy
patches under trees and in shadowy places, but most of it
was gone already. The road was muddy and rutted, and
Ranger picked his way carefully.

A cardinal as red as blood flew past us and a flock of
crows cawed from the treetops, but we saw no one. The
road stretched ahead, winding through fields and in and
out of woods. Not too long ago, we would have passed
farmers with carts, men on horseback, families in carriages, or folks just walking along. Now there was no one.
Not even a soldier.

Over our heads, trees swayed in the wind, making a
sound like a crowd mourning a great loss. Gray clouds
hung low and heavy above the brown fields. Frozen ponds
reflected the dull sky. Not a cow to be seen. Not a sheep.
Not even a squirrel.

"Are we almost there?" Rachel asked after a couple of
hours. "I'm cold and hungry. And my legs hurt from sitting
so long."

I looked to the west. The sun was barely visible through
the clouds, but I could tell it wasn't far above the mountains. It would be dark in less than an hour. "We must be
close," I said.

"I surely hope so. Seems like we've been riding all day," Rachel said wearily.

"Would you rather we were walking?"

"No."

"Well, then."

Rachel sighed and shifted her position. For a while she was silent. The sun slid farther down the sky, lighting the horizon with a long streak of purple. Darkness gathered in the woods, as thick as wool spun from black sheep. The wind rose, rattling in the trees like something trying to break free, moaning every now and then in a woeful way. With all my heart I wished we'd left home earlier.

"You said we'd be there before nightfall." Rachel sounded fearful.

"We will," I said, praying I was right.

Rachel held me tighter. "But, Haswell, the woods look so dark. Will bears eat us?"

"Of course not. They hibernate in the winter. Don't you know anything?" Nonetheless, I touched the butt of the revolver, which I'd stuck in my waistband. It was good to know Rachel and I had some protection. Not from wild animals but men. Deserters, raiders—who knew what manner of person you'd meet so far from houses and towns?

By now we'd reached a bridge I remembered from other trips. I knew that bridge meant we were almost to the farm.

"We're close now, Rachel. Remember that bridge up ahead?"

Rachel hugged me. "Yes, Papa used to pretend it was the bridge at Concord and he'd recite that poem about the shot heard round the world."

I nodded, but for some reason I felt uneasy. The woods

—— 77 ——

on the other side of the bridge were already dark. Tree crowded against tree. Branches intertwined across the road, so it looked like a tunnel leading into the night. A crow cawed and flew out of a tall oak, followed by three or four others. Ruffians, Mama called them, making trouble wherever they went. Outlaws, bandits, thieving rascals.

Ranger slowed, his ears pointed, as if he sensed something, too. I didn't know whether I should urge him forward or rein him in. Could be he was spooked by a shadow or a branch, but he hadn't shown signs of nervousness before.

I leaned close to his head. "What's the matter, fellow?"

Ranger snorted and pawed at the bridge with his front hoof. But he didn't move.

Rachel's grip on me tightened. "Why are we stopping, Haswell?"

"Oh, you know how horses are, Rachel. Sometimes they don't care much for bridges." I nudged Ranger. "Step along, sir. "

Rachel was the first to spy what was bothering Ranger. "Haswell," she cried. "There's someone on the road. See?"

Sure enough, just beyond the bridge a bundle of rags lay in a heap in the mud. Bending over it was a man, desperately pulling at something. He looked up when Rachel spoke. His face was in shadow, but I could see enough of him to tell he was half starved. His hair and beard had grown long and wild and his clothes were nothing but rags.

"I found him first," the man hollered in a half-crazed way. "He's mine. You keep away!"

The man gave a final jerk at the thing and fell backward, clutching a boot in his hands. That's when I realized the heap was a soldier's corpse.

Rachel's grip on me tightened. "It's a dead man, Haswell."

I nodded but kept my eyes on the living man. He was pulling the boots on, forcing his feet into them.

"I get the coat, too," he snarled at me. "And anything else he has on him."

With that, he began pulling at the coat. The dead man rose as if he were fighting to keep what was his, but his head fell back and his arms flapped as the robber succeeded in yanking the coat off. "It stinks," he said with a grimace, "but I'm used to that." He struggled into the coat and stood looking at us. A sadder-looking man never lived and breathed. Nor a scarier one, for that matter.

"You have any food?" He came a little closer, a gaunt man wearing a dead man's boots and coat, reeking of death. But not as old as I'd thought at first.

"Get back." I tried to speak loud, but my voice came out as small as a child's. "Don't come a step closer. I've got a gun and I know how to use it."

Rachel's grip on me tightened and I could feel her trembling. "Go away," she whispered. "Leave us be."

"Ah, now, sweetheart." The man leaned around me, trying to get a better look at my sister. "What's a pretty little girl like you want to be so mean? Ain't your preacher taught you the Lord's way of sharing with the less fortunate?"

Rachel pressed her face against my back. "Make him go away, Haswell."

"All I want is something to eat." The man sounded indignant. "God Almighty, is that too much to ask, boy?"

Instead of answering, I kicked Ranger hard. The horse fairly flew across the bridge, passing the man before he had a chance of stopping us.

"Hey," he hollered after us. "Just a morsel, a sip of water!"

Neither Rachel nor I looked back, but we could hear him shouting and cursing even after we rounded a bend in the road and left him behind.

When we'd gone a safe distance, I slowed the horse to a trot and looked back. Nothing moved among the trees. Nothing followed us.

"Was he a Yankee?" Rachel asked.

"Hard to say. After a while they start looking the same. Dirty, ragged, hungry, sick." Weary of it all, I spit on the ground.

"I think he was a Yankee." Rachel spit on the ground, too. "Were you scared of him, Haswell?"

I hesitated. If I told Rachel the truth, she might worry I wasn't fit to take care of her. "I feared he'd take our food," I said slowly. "But I don't think he aimed to hurt us."

"You could have shot him." Rachel touched the revolver stuck in the waistband of my trousers.

"Yes, but I'm glad I didn't have to."

"Trouble is, folks like us aren't accustomed to killing people," Rachel said with a sigh. "Look how Mama felt after she shot Captain Powell. I wouldn't want you losing your wits, Haswell."

I didn't say anything, so we rode a few minutes in silence. Then Rachel spoke up again. "How do you think Avery feels about killing?"

"He's probably used to it by now, Rachel."

"He just aims and pulls that trigger." Rachel pointed

her finger straight ahead. "Bang! Bang, bang! And he doesn't even know who he hits or whether they die or not."

"I reckon that's just about the way it is." But it made my stomach tight to picture Avery charging into battle like our old hero Achilles, laying waste to the Yankees the way Achilles laid waste to the Trojans. It might change a person to behave like that. What if the souls of all those dead soldiers followed you the rest of your life, rebuking you for killing them? I shivered, and not just because the night was damp and cold. Please God, I prayed, let Avery come home safe, just the way he was when he left. Don't let him be shot or killed or sick.

"I thought we were almost there," Rachel said.

I peered ahead. The road was pale in the dark but criss-crossed with shadows. "I think it's just around that curve," I told her.

When we were finally in sight of the farm, I headed Ranger off the road and into the trees. From the safety of the woods, I peered down at Grandma Colby's house. No smoke rose from the chimney, no lights glowed in the windows. The house was dark against the night sky. Empty. Abandoned. Lifeless. There was no one to welcome us. No one to feed us. No one to tuck us into warm beds.

Rachel squeezed my waist. "Where is Grandma Colby? Where are Aunt Hester and Aunt Esther?" Her voice rose. "Did the Yankees come and kill them?"

"No, of course not." I patted Rachel's knee. "Most likely they've gone to stay with Uncle Cornelius in Winchester." I couldn't help wishing I'd thought of that earlier. As stubborn as Grandma Colby was, she wouldn't stay on the farm with no man to protect her and my aunts.

Rachel sighed. "Oh, Haswell, I'm so hungry and tired and cold."

I slid down from Ranger's back. "Wait here, Rachel. I'll make sure the house is safe. If everything's all right, we can sleep here tonight and go on to Winchester in the morning."

Rachel leaned down and grabbed my arm. "Don't leave me alone in the dark. Suppose that crazy man comes along and steals Ranger from me."

"He's long gone by now," I said, but I couldn't help glancing at the road behind us. Nothing but darkness. No sound but the wind in the trees, no motion except branches tossing.

"Please let me come with you," Rachel begged.

She looked pale in the dim light—scared, too. Not her usual daytime self at all.

"I'll be right back, I promise."

"What if that man kills me?" Rachel called after me. "You'll be sorry then."

"Don't be silly! No one's going to kill you." I turned my back on her and crept off through the trees toward the house. I heard Rachel crying, but she stayed where she was.

Which was a good thing because there was no way of knowing what lay ahead.

◦ 9 ◦

As soon as I was out of Rachel's sight, I took Papa's revolver out of my waistband. Praying I wouldn't have to use it, I slipped from tree to tree along the lane. The ground was frozen, churned up into ruts by horses and wagon wheels and boots. Men had been here, soldiers most likely. North or South, the signs of their presence didn't bode well. They could be renegades, deserters, heartless and greedy. Dangerous.

Instead of going to the front door, I made a wide loop around to the back. A broken rocking chair lay in the mud, along with odds and ends of kitchen things, clothing, and Grandma Colby's favorite carpet, which she claimed had been hand-woven in Persia.

The door lay on the porch, broken off its hinges entirely. I entered cautiously, stopping every now and then to listen. I went from room to room. Most of the furniture was gone. Whether stolen or used for firewood, I couldn't tell. Framed pictures had been yanked from the walls, their glass broken, the faces of my ancestors trampled. In the dim light I stumbled over heaps of silk dresses, shirts and jackets, a tall silk hat Grandfather Colby had worn on fine occasions, bed linens and feather pillows, all torn and soiled and scattered on the floor. But not one person, dead or alive, was to be found.

By the time I rejoined Rachel, a little sliver of moon had just cleared the mountains. I took Ranger's bridle and led him down the lane. Rachel studied me, her face as pale as her doll's in the dusky light.

"Did they kill Grandma Colby and the aunts?" she asked in a quavery voice.

I shook my head. "They wrecked the house, though."

Rachel sighed and hugged Sophia to her chest. But she didn't say a word, just sat on Ranger's back and let me lead him around the house. When I started guiding him up the steps to the open door, Rachel stared at me as if I'd taken leave of my senses. "Haswell, you can't take this horse into Grandma Colby's house."

"He can't make it any worse than it already is," I said. "Besides, he needs shelter, too. What if that lunatic found him outside? He'd be on his back in a second."

Rachel frowned and slid off Ranger's back. "I thought you said he was far from here, miles away."

"Well, I hope he is," I said, "but who knows who could come sneaking around in the dark?"

Without looking at Rachel, I tied Ranger to the stair rail in the hall and took off his saddle. From one of the saddlebags, I pulled out a handful of the oats. While Ranger munched his food, I went out to the well and pumped water for him and us. Two bucketfuls. Then I set myself to finding furniture to use for a fire. Whoever had been here hadn't taken much from the second floor. I began with doors and shutters and old odds and ends of furniture.

I lacked the heart to burn a pair of carved chairs and a small walnut table. According to Mama, Grandfather Colby had brought them from Richmond as a wedding present for Grandma Colby.

Using an ax I found in the kitchen, I split the doors and shutters into kindling wood. Rachel watched silently. After a while she said, "Grandma Colby's going to skin you alive for breaking up her belongings."

"I wasn't the one who wrecked the house. What difference do a few more things make?"

Rachel looked around the ruins of Grandma Colby's once fine home. "Mama thought Grandma Colby was house-proud," she said. "Now she's got nothing left to be proud of."

I shrugged and tossed a kitchen chair leg into the fireplace. Mama had been right. Grandma Colby had taken great delight in showing off her fine drapes and wallpaper from France, her mahogany, her silver, her silks and satins and fine china from England.

If she weren't such a mean old lady, I would've felt sorry for her, but she'd made Mama feel bad by blaming our so-called poverty on Papa. Grandma Colby faulted him for being more interested in history and poetry than acquiring wealth.

No matter what she said, none of us had ever felt poor. We had clothes on our backs, food in our bellies, a roof over our head, and all we needed.

But not anymore. No, not anymore. Hard Times had knocked so hard on our door, he'd broken it down.

When I'd piled up the proper amount of furniture parts, I struggled to light the fire. It took a while, but I finally got it going. The chimney drew fine and soon the room warmed up. Rachel and I crouched near the flames and ate the vegetables we'd brought from home.

After we'd eaten all we had, we gathered blankets and pillows and made ourselves beds by the fireplace. For a while neither of us spoke. We lay there watching the fire turn the wood to glowing coals and ashes. Every now and then I added more fuel, but I knew it would burn out long before morning.

"It looks like cities burning," Rachel said. "Farms, and barns, and houses, all burning, burning, burning." She buried her face in her arms. "I used to love watching fire," she added softly, "but that was before the war."

Feeling much the same, I closed my eyes and let the fire warm my back. Half asleep, I remembered Papa talking about ancient wars and how the Greeks looted Troy and burned it and how the great Trojan Aeneas fled his homeland, carrying his father on his back, and founded the Roman Empire. And then a long while later the barbarians came and burned Rome. It seemed people had done nothing but loot and burn since the beginning of time. God wouldn't need to destroy the world with fire. We'd most likely beat Him to it.

◆

I woke in the morning cold and stiff from sleeping on the floor. The fire was out, and the smell of wood smoke hung in the air. When I sat up, Rachel opened her eyes. For a moment, she looked bewildered, as if she had no idea where she was. Then she remembered.

"What are we going to do now?" she asked.

I got to my feet, still wrapped in the blanket, and went to the window. The sky was a dull, solid gray, as lifeless as the ashes of last night's fire.

"Why, I guess we'll go on to Winchester," I said.

"Winchester." Rachel sighed. "That's a long way, Haswell. I'm still sore from yesterday." She patted her rear end and gave me a pleading look. "Can't we just stay one more night here?"

"It's only a day's ride, Rachel."

She poked out her lower lip and folded her arms across her chest. "My fanny's too sore to get on that horse."

"What if the soldiers come back?"

Her eyes widened. "Do you think they will?"

"They might."

Without another complaint, Rachel gathered up her blankets and her doll and went outside to use the outhouse.

I fed Ranger the last of his oats and led him out into the gray dawn. He tossed his head and nickered as if he were glad to be outside again. Rachel emerged from the outhouse, clutching Sophia and trailing her blankets. I boosted her onto Ranger's back, helped her wrap herself up warm, and climbed into the saddle. My rear end was tender, too, but I wasn't about to admit it.

We paused at the top of the hill and stared down at the farm. Except for the barn, the place didn't look too bad. At least the house was still standing. Maybe someday Grandma Colby would come back. But then again, maybe she wouldn't. Who would help her plant crops and rebuild things? Papa was dead. Uncle Cornelius was a city man, a lawyer. His son, John, was two years dead, killed at Gettysburg. And Avery and I would have our own farm to work on.

We rode in and out of cold showers, passing one deserted farm after another. General Sheridan had done his work well. Now and then we'd meet a solitary man or woman trudging grimly through the mud, head down, bundled in blankets like us, tired and hungry like us.

Other times it might be a family pulling a cart loaded with furniture, sometimes with the help of a gaunt horse or an ox, but usually just themselves. Small children with pale, hungry faces walked along beside the carts. Worn-down mothers carried babies in their arms. Haggard fathers gave orders. Most had little to say but "Good day." Some didn't even say that much. I guessed they were too wrapped up in worries of their own to notice anyone else.

"Where do you suppose they're all going?" Rachel asked.

"I reckon they have family somewhere, like us."

"But most of them are heading away from Winchester." Rachel sounded worried. "Have you noticed that, Haswell?"

I'd heard Winchester had been in Yankee hands since fall. What with General Sheridan taking all he could for his own troops, it had been a bad winter for the people there. Since Rachel and I had no choice but to continue, we kept on walking against the stream of refugees.

A man walking along beside a cart full of children and furniture stopped to ask, "You children surely ain't heading for Winchester, are you?"

"Yes, sir, in fact we are. We have family there."

"The general's set hisself up in the best house in town. We got nothing there. No food. No shelter."

Another fellow spoke up. "Those that collaborate do right well, taking Yankees into their homes and getting food and drink in return."

"Ain't that the truth." The first man spit on the ground beside his wagon. "You think your kin would take in a Yankee?"

"No, sir, they would not." I was mortally offended he'd ask such a question. "My father died in Richmond and my brother's in Petersburg."

"Yankees burned our house and killed our mother," Rachel added, her face pinched white with fury.

Hearing this, the man's wife leaned out of the cart. She was holding a little baby to her breast. "We're heading toward Richmond," she told us. "You children want to come along? There's no telling what you'll find in Winchester."

"Thank you, ma'am, but my sister and I promised our mother we'd go to our grandmother."

"Well, God help you and bless you, children, and keep you safe." The woman drew back into the cart. I heard the baby crying as the cart went on its way.

Since neither of us could think of anything else to do, we rode on toward Winchester. If the truth be told, I felt a sight more heart heavy than I had when we'd left Grandma Colby's farm. I was weak from hunger and weary from worrying. The constant swaying motion of Ranger's walk threatened to put me to sleep. My eyes would close and then jerk open.

I guess my drowsiness dulled my attention, for all of a sudden a gaunt and raggedy man appeared from nowhere. I hoped to get past him without trouble, but he stood in the middle of the road, blocking our way and staring at me with those same burned-out eyes I'd seen before.

"That's a fine-looking horse you got there, boy." He was looking sharp at me, gauging my mettle, I reckoned.

"Yes, siree, mighty fine." The man stretched out a dirty hand, more bone than flesh, and stroked Ranger's neck. The horse's muscles twitched. The stranger reeked of filth and I could see lice crawling in his hair. His ragged clothes gave him the look of a scarecrow who'd been left out in the field too long.

"It's a shame to see a horse like him wasted on a puny boy and girl," he added.

I nudged Ranger, but the man tightened his grip on the bridle. "I've come a long way, boy," he said. "Walked the soles off my boots twice. What I could use now is a good horse. You and that there gal get down from the horse and won't nobody get hurt."

I pushed my jacket aside to reveal Papa's revolver sticking out of my trousers. "Leave us be."

The man hesitated. "Now, I call that a right unfriendly attitude." He grinned and reached into his pocket. "Why, I got a thousand Confederate dollars I'll give for the horse. Think what that would buy."

I pulled out the revolver and cocked it. "No, sir," I told him. "This horse isn't for sale. Now let go of him and let us pass."

The man studied my face. "You ain't got the stomach for killing, boy."

From behind me, Rachel spoke up. "Don't you dare take our horse. My brother has already killed three men who tried to steal him."

The man peered around me to see Rachel, and I brought the revolver's handle down on his head as hard as I could. Pain shot up my arm and I almost dropped my weapon. The man went down hard. I didn't wait to find out if I'd killed him. I kicked Ranger hard. Off he went at full gallop, leaving the man sprawled in the road.

While Rachel congratulated herself for coming up with a good lie at just the right moment, I thought about what the man had said. He'd been right. I had no more stomach for killing than Mama.

·10·

WE REACHED THE OUTSKIRTS of Winchester early in the evening. It was clear the fighting had been fierce since the last time I'd seen the town. Fine old houses lay in ruins. The tall maples lining the streets were scarred and scorched, some snapped off like matchsticks. Broken carts and carriages littered the roadsides. The smell of smoke and old fires lingered in the chilly air.

To the west, just over the mountains, the sun sank into a lake of crimson fire, making the whole scene a vision of hell. Here and there a person walked about the streets. Most moved furtively, looking about with every step they took.

I reckoned they were fearful of encountering Yankee soldiers. Feeling apprehensive myself, I followed their lead and kept alert for danger.

Just as I reached a corner, two Yankee soldiers came around it from the other direction. At the sight of Rachel and me, they stopped short. One pulled a revolver and told us to stay where we were.

I reined in Ranger. "Yes, sir," I said, doing my best to sound polite.

Rachel clung to me, too surprised to say a word, which I counted as a blessing. If she got sassy, there was no telling what might become of us.

"Where do you think you're going?" one of the men asked. "It's more than an hour past curfew for Rebels."

"Curfew?" I stared at the soldier as if I didn't know the meaning of the word.

"No Rebels are allowed in the street after five o'clock," the other said. "The church bell rang six twenty minutes ago."

"But we just got here, sir. We didn't know about the curfew. We never meant to break the law."

"We're going to our uncle's house," Rachel added. "He's an important lawyer, and you'll be sorry if you—"

"Forgive my sister," I said loudly. "She's just so tired and so hungry. We've ridden all day to get here and—"

"What's your uncle's name?" the soldier with the gun asked.

"Mr. Cornelius Colby. He lives on Bank Street."

The two bent their heads together and talked in voices too low for me to catch the words.

Rachel pinched my arm. "Why are you acting like a coward? Those Yankees have no right to—"

I turned and glared at her. "Hush! You want to get us thrown in jail?"

Rachel shrank back and shook her head.

The soldier with the gun waved us on. "Go straight to Mr. Colby's house. If I see you out past curfew again, I'll shoot you."

"Yes, sir." As I rode away, I heard them laughing. I figured they'd amused themselves by scaring us.

"Yankee devils!" Rachel called back at them, but if they heard her, they took no notice.

At last we came to Uncle Cornelius's street. The houses were in good shape, as if the battles had swept the other way and spared them. Rachel saw the lighted windows first.

"Thank the Lord," she whispered. "Uncle Cornelius is home."

"Wait under this tree, Rachel, till I make sure it's safe. For all we know, Yankees are occupying the house."

Rachel stuck out her lip, but she did as I said, just as she'd done the night before. "You come right back," she said. "Don't forget me."

Uncle Cornelius's house sat on a slight rise of ground, surrounded by a green lawn big enough for a cornfield. Even in the dim light of evening, I could see weeds flourishing, as well as wheel ruts and churned-up ground. The house itself was badly in need of paint but otherwise intact.

I crept to a window and peered in. There was Uncle Cornelius, a bit stouter than I recalled, sitting by the fire. Across the room from him, Grandma Colby perched on the sofa, flanked by Aunt Hester and Aunt Esther, all three a bit shabbier than usual but seeming to be healthy enough. Grandma Colby looked smaller, though, as if the war and its losses had shrunk her. Identical in plain gray dresses, the aunts sat up straight, their hair pulled back tightly from their narrow faces. All three women kept their heads down and busied themselves with their embroidery.

What drew my attention away from them was the guest. In the place of honor sat a Union officer, wearing a dandy blue uniform fastened with shiny gold buttons. His whiskers were neatly trimmed, and his belly shook with laughter at a story Uncle Cornelius was telling. In one hand he held a brandy glass and in the other a pipe. Uncle Cornelius had brandy and a pipe as well.

Grandma Colby and the aunts sipped tea from delicate porcelain cups. The aunts' faces were expressionless, but Grandma Colby wore her usual frown, which seemed to be directed at both Uncle Cornelius and the major. It was clear *she* hadn't invited a Yankee into the house.

I hurried back to Rachel. "They're entertaining an officer from the Union Army, but I believe it's safe to knock at the door."

"There's a *Yankee* in there?" Rachel stared at me as if I'd told her our uncle was entertaining the devil himself.

"I don't like it any better than you do. But I'm cold and tired and hungry, and I want some food in my belly and a warm place to sleep."

Rachel pouted while I tied Ranger to a hitching post by the side of the house, but she didn't say another word about the Yankee officer. Lord knew what she was thinking. Or planning. For safety's sake, I said, "Don't say a word about Captain Powell or this horse."

"I'm not a simpleton." Rachel followed me up the wide brick steps to the front door. "Do you think they've already eaten supper?" she whispered.

"Most likely, but maybe they have leftovers." It reassured me somewhat to hear her mention supper. Perhaps she was too hungry to risk insulting anyone.

On the door above my head, a fierce brass lion's head with a heavy ring in its mouth scowled down at me. It had frightened me when I was little, mainly because Avery told me it might come to life and eat me up. I was younger than Rachel at the time. Now I lifted the ring and let it fall with a thump. Things like door knockers no longer scared me.

No one came. I knocked louder. After the third try, Aunt Hester opened the door a crack and peered down at us.

"You children go away," she said. "I'm sorry, truly I am, but we can't feed you. We have nothing to spare, my dears."

Before she could close the door, Rachel cried out, "Aunt Hester, it's Haswell and me. Surely you won't turn your own kin away!"

Aunt Hester paused, her face confused. From the parlor, Grandma Colby called, "Hester, we can't feed every beggar in town. Tell them to be on their way, or I'll come and do it for you!"

"But, Mother—"

Rachel didn't wait for our aunt to finish her sentence. Without another word, she pushed past the befuddled woman, and I followed her. The house was warm and so full of good smells, I almost swooned.

Rachel walked straight into the parlor and stopped in front of Grandma Colby. "Please don't send us away," she begged. "Mama told us to come to you. We went to your farm and you weren't there, so we came to Winchester, all because Mama said you'd take care of us." She gave Grandma Colby a pleading look. "If you don't want us, where are we to go?"

Everyone in the parlor stared at us. I suppose we were a sight. Unwashed, uncombed, dressed in rags, and most likely smelling more like pigs than roses. Mama and Papa would have been ashamed to claim us as theirs.

"It's Rachel and Haswell, Mother." Aunt Hester twisted and untwisted her pale hands, obviously fearing Grandma Colby's anger for letting urchins into the house. "Rebecca's children."

Grandma Colby beckoned us closer. Her sight was poor, but she'd never admit it. While everyone, including the major, watched, she studied Rachel and me. "Where is your mother?" she asked. "Rebecca is sadly remiss in domestic matters, but I've never known her to neglect her children."

Rachel burst into tears. "Mama's dead. She took fever after the Yankees came." She flung herself at Grandma Colby, plainly expecting to be comforted.

Grandma Colby's face wrinkled in distaste, and she pushed Rachel away. Holding the weeping girl at arm's length, she cried, "What do you mean, Rebecca's dead?"

I put my arms round Rachel and let her cry all over my jacket. "The Yankees burned our house to the ground," I told Grandma Colby. "Mama took fever. Before she died, she told us to come to you, so we did." I stared at her steadily while I spoke, keeping my voice firm and my eyes dry. I didn't once look at the Union officer, but I wanted him to hear every word.

Grandma Colby gasped and pressed a hand to her heart. "Rebecca . . . dead? The house burned?" She turned to Uncle Cornelius. "Can it be true?"

Uncle Cornelius looked at me. "I've known Haswell to be a mischievous sort, but I've never known him to lie, Mother."

Grandma Colby clasped her hands tight and shut her eyes. "Oh, Rebecca, Rebecca, my poor dear Rebecca."

The aunts gathered round their mother and tried to comfort her, but she pushed their fluttering hands aside. "Leave me be, leave me be," she sobbed. "God in heaven, will there ever be an end to this misery?"

The Yankee cleared his throat. "The men were most likely renegades of some sort. Deserters. I regret to say the army cannot restrain such villains."

I turned to the man. "They were cavalrymen from Pennsylvania. They came to our house because they were looking for one of Mosby's men."

"Oh, good God." The officer lowered his bushy eyebrows. "John Singleton Mosby is a grievous nuisance—a scourge, a devil." He paused and drew on his pipe, then leaned toward me. "Were their suspicions correct? Were you hiding one of that rogue's accursed Bushwhackers?"

"James Marshall came to us wounded and sick. We took him in, and Mama restored his health. Now, thanks to your men, both James Marshall and Mama are dead."

While I spoke, my heart pounded hard and my breath came and went, fast and shallow. I didn't know why a Union officer was in my uncle's house or why he seemed so friendly and familiar with him. I glanced at Uncle Cornelius, hoping he'd denounce the Yankees, but he just sat there, twirling his brandy glass and gazing at the amber liquid as if it held the answers to life's mysteries. In my uncle's eyes, I'd clearly gone too far.

"The soldiers simply followed orders," the officer said. "General Sheridan has mandated strong reprisals against those who shelter Bushwhackers."

He looked at Uncle Cornelius and took a long pull on his pipe. "It's unfortunate the children's mother died," he added in a pious voice, "but it wasn't Yankee soldiers who killed her. Perhaps she would have died of fever even if the men hadn't come to the house."

Rachel drew in her breath as if to speak. I squeezed her arm as gently as I could, knowing a pinch would result in a screech. She looked at me, and I shook my head. Fortunately, she remembered what I'd told her about Mama and Captain Powell and kept her mouth shut.

Taking advantage of the silence, Uncle Cornelius said, "Children, it seems I've neglected my manners. This is Major Thomas Dennison. He's with the Union Army. We are privileged to share our home with him."

The major rose to his feet. He was a tall, heavy-set man with a rosy complexion, showing none of the usual sickness and pallor of a typical soldier on either side. His well-polished gold buttons twinkled in the firelight, and so did the gold fillings in his teeth.

As Uncle Cornelius introduced me, Major Dennison held out his hand. I kept my hands in my pockets. Damned if I'd shake the hand of my enemy.

A little silence fell, and the major's face reddened. "God Almighty, boy, have you no manners?" he asked.

"Manners have nothing to do with it," I said, keeping my eyes on his. Once again my heart was pounding, both harder and faster this time.

"Please excuse my nephew, Thomas," Uncle Cornelius said to the major. "He's come a long way, without much food or rest from the looks of him."

"Neither fatigue nor hunger is an excuse for rudeness," the major said. "Were he one of my soldiers, I'd have him flogged."

With that and a scowl for me, Major Dennison went to the sideboard and refilled his brandy glass. With his back turned to the room, he added, "I heard Southerners had the manners of aristocrats, but, like many other rumors, I find it to be false in most cases."

Uncle Cornelius beckoned to the aunts. "Perhaps you two could wash these children," he whispered. "Feed them. Put them to bed. Get them out of the major's sight."

"Yes," Grandma Colby said, "that's a fine idea. I'm going to retire myself. Rebecca's death is one grief too many." Gripping her cane, the old woman levered herself off the sofa and hobbled toward the stairs. Her back bent more than I recalled, and she walked more slowly. Gone were the days when she had the energy to chase me around the yard with a switch in her hand.

"Don't forget to bathe them," she told the aunts. To Rachel and me, she said. "I am truly sorry to hear of your mother's death. Despite her unfortunate marriage, I was very fond of Rebecca." Up the stairs she went, one slow step at a time, raising each foot as if her shoes were made of lead. We watched till she reached the top and headed down the hall to her room.

· 11 ·

As soon as the kitchen door swung shut behind us, the aunts turned to me. "Oh, Haswell, you should have taken Major Dennison's hand," Aunt Esther said.

Aunt Hester nodded. "Esther is right. We both understand how you feel, but we are greatly beholden to Major Dennison."

"Beholden to a Yankee?" I stared at the aunts. "I'd sooner be beholden to Lucifer himself!"

Both aunts gasped. "Haswell, what would your poor dear mother say if she could hear you speak so?" Aunt Hester asked.

At the sound of Mama's name, Rachel's eyes filled with tears. She pressed Sophie to her skinny little breast, a silent picture of the misery I was holding inside.

Aunt Esther reached out and patted Rachel's shoulder, as if she were befriending a stray dog that might bite. "Oh, now, Rachel," she whispered. "Please don't cry, darling."

Aunt Hester left Aunt Esther to comfort Rachel as best she could. Turning to me, she murmured, "Please don't be rude to the major, Haswell."

I studied my aunt's worried face. She and her twin were quiet, peaceable sorts, not given to anger or complaint. Had they been contentious, they could never have lived with Grandma Colby all these years. But it was more than my bad manners that bothered Aunt Hester.

"Why do you care what I say to a Yankee major?" I asked. "What's he doing here anyway?"

Lowering her voice to a whisper, she said, "The major's been quartered with us, Haswell."

"He *lives* here?"

The aunts nodded and glanced almost fearfully at the closed kitchen door. Behind it, we could hear the major laughing at something Uncle Cornelius had said. "You see," Aunt Hester went on, "Winchester's under martial law. Officers are quartered in houses all over town."

"Those homes that are still standing, that is," Aunt Esther put in softly.

"Yes," Aunt Hester agreed. "That's why we must be gracious to Major Dennison. If he takes our behavior amiss, he might brand us traitors and burn our house, too."

"Are you saying Uncle Cornelius is a collaborator?" I asked. "His own son died fighting in Lee's army. And Avery's still in the war, doing his best for the South. How can he—"

"Hush, Haswell!" Aunt Hester's voice was as sharp as a slap. "You heard what I told you."

Rachel looked at the aunts wearily, her eyes red, her dirty face streaked with tears. "I hate this war," she said in a small, dry voice.

Much as I once craved honor and glory, I was beginning to agree. Of course, I never would have admitted to it, not even under the most fearsome torture ever devised. But so far it seemed all the war had done was destroy everything I loved. Mama and Papa. The Valley itself. And for what? For what? So the major could sit in Uncle Cornelius's house polishing his gold buttons and stuffing his belly and scaring the poor aunts half silly?

"Now, why don't you go and wash, Haswell." Aunt Hester rose to her feet and began stirring something in a pot. "You and Rachel need some food in your bellies."

The smell of whatever was on the stove cheered Rachel. Wiping her eyes, she said, "We're truly on the verge of starvation."

Aunt Esther smiled at Aunt Hester. "That child always has had the most dramatic way of expressing herself. 'On the verge of starvation,' indeed."

"Indeed," Hester agreed.

The talk of starvation reminded me of Ranger, waiting patiently in the cold for his oats. "Excuse me a minute," I said to the aunts, "but my horse needs feed and shelter. Do you have room for him in the stable?"

"There's an extra stall and plenty of oats," Aunt Hester said. "The major keeps his horse there, too."

Ranger nickered when he saw me coming. I took his bridle and stroked his nose. "Sorry, sir, but I was detained inside by one of your kind, a Union major. Not that I hold it against you."

The stable was warm and smelled of fodder and the sweet sweat of horses. I breathed it in deep, recalling the smell of our stable and the sound of Papa talking gentle to the horses while they munched their oats. I pressed my face against Ranger's warm side and wept for Papa and Mama and James Marshall and our farm.

It was the first time I'd let myself cry. The grief came from so deep inside it hurt my belly and my chest and my throat. For a while it seemed I'd never stop. I guessed Rachel was lucky in some ways to be a girl. She could cry whenever she liked. But it didn't do for me to cry. I was almost a man.

When I'd finally used up my tears, I left Ranger eating his bucket of oats. In a nearby stall, a sorry-looking dapple gray watched me pass. Its condition didn't say much for the major's horsemanship.

"What were you doing out there so long?" Rachel asked me. "The aunts said I couldn't eat till you came back."

"Just taking care of Ranger." I washed my hands at the sink and dropped into a chair. I kept my head down so no one would see I'd been crying.

The aunts busied themselves filling plates with leftovers. From the look of the potatoes, ham, beets, and biscuits, the folks in this house weren't feeling the war pinch their bellies. I reckoned it paid to quarter a Yankee officer. But I myself wouldn't have done it. No, not for the best beef in the country.

While we said grace, Rachel stared at her food as if she feared it would vanish like magic. The second we said "Amen," I dug in, glad it was real and just as good as it looked. My sister followed my example.

"Now, now, children," Aunt Esther said. "There's no need to wolf your supper. You'll make yourselves sick."

"The poor things," Aunt Hester murmured. "They must truly be famished."

Aunt Esther reached out and patted our arms. "We're so sorry for your suffering," she said. "I know how much you miss your mother and father. But you'll be safe here. We'll provide for you, keep you warm and safe."

Aunt Hester nodded her head. "That's what families are for. To take care of each other."

Rachel stared at Aunt Hester, a forkful of ham halfway

to her mouth. "Grandma Colby won't send us to an orphanage, will she?"

"An orphanage?" Aunt Hester sounded shocked. "Good gracious, child, whatever gave you such an idea?"

Rachel lowered her fork and gazed from one aunt to the other. "Grandma Colby didn't like Papa," she said in a low voice. "Maybe she doesn't like Haswell and me, either."

"You are both Rebecca's children," Aunt Esther spoke up. "That means you are blood kin. Colbys don't neglect family."

"Never have," Aunt Hester agreed. "Never will."

Aunt Esther leaned toward me. "Do you recall old Uncle John? Why, he hadn't any sense at all, but Father kept him till he died. He wandered all over and folks brought him home like a stray cow."

"Some people would have sent him to the poor farm," Aunt Hester added, "Uncle John was a nuisance—but he was family."

Rachel turned to me, her eyes wide. "Do you remember him, Haswell?"

A picture came to mind of a scary old man sitting in a rocking chair. He never said anything that made sense, though sometimes he spoke up loud and clear about Judgment Day. He'd scared me with talk of the world burning to a cinder and sinners being cast headlong into hell.

"He was old—the oldest man alive," I told Rachel. "Beard down to his toes almost. He died when you were a baby."

Rachel nodded, her eyes half closed, her head drooping over her empty plate. "I was a pretty baby," she said, half asleep already. "Mama said so. I was the girl she was hoping for. And Papa agreed."

She yawned, and I found myself yawning, too. My eyelids felt weighted, and I wasn't sure I could stay awake much longer.

Aunt Hester glanced at Aunt Esther. "I think it's time these poor children went to bed."

"Shouldn't we wash them first?" Aunt Hester asked.

"Oh, I think that can wait till morning. Just look at them. They can't keep their eyes open, either one."

Aunt Hester frowned at her sister. "You heard what Mother said."

"I guess we'd better do it, then." Aunt Esther smiled apologetically and helped her sister heat water on the stove. By the time the tub was full and the curtain drawn round it, Rachel was sound asleep and I was close to it.

Aunt Esther woke Rachel as gently as possible and gave her a good washing, hair and all. When she was done, I bathed in the same water, the way we always did. Though it mortified me, Aunt Hester insisted on scrubbing me. While she worked on me, I heard Rachel fussing about the way Aunt Esther combed out the tangles in her hair.

Just about the time Rachel stopped complaining, Aunt Esther thrust aside the curtain. "Haswell, what are you doing with this?" She held my revolver the way a person holds a dead rat by the tail.

Forgetting my modesty, I leapt to my feet, sloshing water everywhere, and grabbed my gun. Sitting back down, I said, "It's mine and I need it. Where did you find it?"

Alarmed by my bad manners, both aunts stepped away from me. "It fell out of your trousers when I was gathering your dirty clothes." Aunt Esther eyed the revolver uneasily. "It doesn't seem right for a boy to be carrying something like that. It's a lethal weapon."

"Why, it could kill somebody," Aunt Hester added.

I gripped the revolver tighter. "I need it."

The aunts looked at each other, all flustered. "Well, now, Haswell—" Aunt Esther began and then turned to her twin sister. "What should we do, Hester?"

Hester bit her lip. "Why, Esther, I just don't know. Corny wouldn't want the boy carrying a weapon."

"Don't tell Uncle Cornelius," I begged. "This gun belonged to Papa. He wanted me to have it." That wasn't literally true, but if Papa knew my circumstances, he would want me to have it.

The aunts considered, looking at me, looking at each other. Rachel appeared and got her piece in. "Papa would be angry if Uncle Cornelius took that gun from Haswell."

"Well," Aunt Esther said, "I guess there's no harm in your having a keepsake of your father's."

Aunt Hester nodded. "Just keep it out of sight, Haswell. And all these bullets, too." She held up a handful she'd removed from my other pocket.

"Yes, ma'am," I promised. "I'll hide it all away, and no one will be the wiser."

Aunt Hester handed me Rachel's damp towel, and Aunt Esther laid a nightshirt over the back of the chair. "You dry yourself," she said. "As soon as you're decent, we'll show you your bedroom. "

The aunts withdrew and the curtain fell back into place. I dried quickly and slipped the nightshirt over my head. It was of more than ample size so I hid the revolver and its ammunition in a fold of cloth and joined Rachel and the aunts.

"Don't you two look beautiful!" Aunt Hester said, smiling at the two of us decked out in borrowed nightclothes.

Rachel's flannel gown trailed behind her, both longer and bigger than mine.

"All clean and fresh and ready to be tucked into bed." Aunt Hester smiled broadly and gave us each a small kiss.

"Come this way." Aunt Esther led us to the back stairs, the ones usually reserved for servants. "We don't want to disturb Corny and the major."

"Or Mother," Aunt Hester added. "She sleeps so light. The slightest noise wakes her. A mouse creeping across the floor. A creaking step. A cough, a snore."

The aunts took Rachel to a small guest room. Before she left me, Rachel handed me James Marshall's letter. "It fell out of your trousers, too. Good thing I saw it, or it would be burned up in the fire by now."

"What's that?" Aunt Hester asked.

"A letter I promised to mail."

Aunt Esther held out her hand. "I'll see to it, Haswell," she said, "though I can't guarantee the postman will be able to decipher the writing. The ink's faded and the envelope is filthy."

I held on to the letter. "No, thank you, Aunt. I have to write something to go along with it."

"James Marshall wrote it," Rachel put in. "It's for his father, but Haswell wants to say how James Marshall was killed by the Yankees."

Aunt Esther turned to Aunt Hester. "Why, sister, that seems the proper thing to do."

Aunt Hester agreed, and the two of them showed me to my cousin John's old room. The first thing I did when they left was hide the revolver and the bullets, as well as James Marshall's letter, under the mattress. Then I crawled into the big soft bed.

Tired as I was, being in John's room saddened me. The news of his death at Gettysburg had brought on Aunt Caroline's death, Mama had said, for she'd died the very next month, still in mourning for her only child.

I reckoned Uncle Cornelius was in mourning himself, which made it all the harder to understand his getting so chummy with a Yankee officer. But then I recalled Papa's saying Uncle Cornelius treasured his comfort above all else. He loved good food and fine wine. He smoked the best cigars and enjoyed card games and horse racing. Much as it disgusted me, it seemed my uncle was willing to consort with the enemy if it meant living the good life he was accustomed to.

The wind tugged at a loose shutter, bang, bang, banging it against the side of the house. It was a haunting, knocking sound. I shivered under the warm covers, for it occurred to me John was buried somewhere out there in the dark and cold. Suppose the wind was his spirit at the window, knocking to come in and lie in the bed where I now lay?

To drive my fearsome thoughts away, I forced myself to think about John's summer visits. He and Avery used to swim across the river down at the farm, racing each other. John always won. He was three years older than Avery, and that was definitely to his advantage. He'd stand on the bank and crow like a rooster. Avery would holler, "Just wait till next time. I'll beat you yet!" And then they'd wrestle and fool around.

I was little at the time, too puny to swim across the river, but I used to imagine myself getting bigger and beating John. Then I'd have my chance to crow.

Now those days seemed like a hundred years ago.

·12·

THE NEXT DAY I WOKE thinking I was at home in my own bed looking at the tiny blue pineapples on my wallpaper. A second later I remembered. I was in Uncle Cornelius's house in a room papered just like mine. Mama and Aunt Caroline had chosen that pattern together, Mama had told me. I shut my eyes against the sunlight streaming through the window. It seemed I saw reminders of Mama everywhere I looked.

I didn't have long to lie there. Rachel came bounding into the room and jumped on my bed. "It's time to wake up, Haswell!" she cried. "Don't you smell hoecakes cooking? And grits? Coffee, too."

She looked lost in a dress obviously owned by a bigger person, but her face was clean and her hair was neatly braided. Mama would have been pleased to see the color in her cheeks.

I sat up and sniffed. Though it hardly seemed possible, I smelled what my sister smelled. My stomach woke up with a growl that made Rachel giggle.

When her stomach answered mine, she laughed harder. "Our bellies are talking to each other, Haswell!"

"And I know what they're saying." I reached for a pair of trousers Aunt Esther had laid out the night before.

They'd belonged to John and were a bit long in the leg and wide in the seat, but at least they were in one piece.

Rachel grinned. "They're saying, 'Let's go eat!'"

Pulling up the suspenders, I ran down the hall after her, both of us laughing and shouting about who'd eat the most. Ahead of us a door opened and a voice bellowed, "Good God! You are totally unschooled in proper behavior!"

The major stepped into the hall and blocked our way. "Some people enjoy a few extra hours of sleep in the morning! They don't expect their slumber to be disturbed by a pair of rude children caterwauling outside the door."

Rachel and I looked as surly as we dared. Before either of us could think of an appropriate answer, the aunts came bustling up the steps and down the hall toward us.

"Oh, Major Dennison . . . " Aunt Esther began.

". . . we're so sorry you were disturbed," Aunt Hester continued.

"The children meant no harm," said Aunt Esther.

"They're just high-spirited," Aunt Hester agreed.

Aunt Esther nodded. "Like colts in the spring, frisking their little selves in the pasture."

"Well, let them frisk their little selves in somebody else's pasture," the major snapped. "Never have liked children. Perhaps I can find rooms more to my liking elsewhere."

"Oh, major, I do assure you it will not be necessary to move," Aunt Hester said, her face anxious.

"Haswell and Rachel won't awaken you again," Aunt Esther added, equally anxious.

"Isn't that true?" Aunt Hester asked us, skewering our consciences with a pleading look.

Though I'm sure Rachel wanted to disturb the major

even more than I did, we nodded our heads solemnly. "Yes, ma'am," we chorused.

"I advise you to keep your word." With that, Major Dennison withdrew to his room and shut the door.

As we followed the aunts downstairs to the kitchen, Aunt Esther begged us to avoid annoying the major. "I told you last night what will happen if the major leaves."

"Why, we'd starve to death before spring," Aunt Hester put in. "And this house would end up as quarters for the infantry. You can imagine how they'd treat it. And us."

With that, Aunt Hester placed a steaming plate of hoecakes right under my nose. "Eat all you want, Haswell. You need to put some flesh on those big bones of yours."

"Yes, indeed." Aunt Esther thumped a pitcher down. "And pour some of this good molasses on them."

I gave in to the weakness of the flesh and heaped hoecakes on my plate, just about drowning them in molasses. Shamed as I am to admit it, I enjoyed my second helping just as much as I'd enjoyed my first. Which proves Isaiah to be one of the wisest of the prophets, for didn't he say, "Everyone is a hypocrite and an evil doer"?

After I'd eaten, I went out to the stable to feed Ranger. When he saw me coming, he raised his head and nickered sweetly, which made me feel good all over. An animal's greeting is something to value. Not one of them is a hypocrite—except perhaps for cats who only act friendly when they're hungry.

I sat down in the stall and watched Ranger eat, loving the sound he made chomping on his oats. When he'd finished, I began currying him. His coat had been sadly neglected. By the time I was done, he looked like a different animal, shiny and sleek, a handsome beast with the lines of a Thoroughbred.

I was so absorbed in admiring Ranger, I didn't hear the major until he coughed. I whirled around to see him leaning on the gate of the stall, studying Ranger as if he'd never seen a horse before.

"Where did you get that fine animal?" he asked me.

I thought fast. "Papa gave him to me on my thirteenth birthday," I said, borrowing James Marshall's story about his horse. I knew he wouldn't mind.

"Is that right?" Major Dennison kept on studying Ranger. "I have the oddest feeling I've seen him somewhere."

His words gave me a shiver. What if he'd known Captain Powell? "There's lots of fine chestnuts about," I said, keeping my voice steady. "I reckon many of them resemble Ranger."

Major Dennison took his pipe out of his pocket and lit it. He never took his eyes off Ranger except to blink. "Not many as fine as this one," he said slowly.

I smoothed Ranger's flanks with the curry brush. "I'm lucky to have him."

The major pulled on his pipe. "You know, I don't see you as the sort of boy whose father could afford a horse like this. Your uncle told me last night your papa was better at philosophizing than farming. Your grandma didn't approve of your mother marrying him. Did her best to talk her out of it."

I swallowed hard. "Truth to tell," I said slowly, "Papa won this horse in a card game." Lies were coming easier and easier, proving I was indeed an evildoer as well as a hypocrite. Mama would be ashamed of me. And so would Papa, who valued honesty above all virtues in this sinful world. What's more, he'd never played a game of cards in his entire life.

"A philosopher and a card player." The major exhaled a cloud of sweet-smelling smoke. "My, my. No wonder he wasn't too good at farming."

With all my heart I wished the major had business to do instead of standing here in the stable staring at Ranger and me.

"There wasn't anything wrong with Papa's farming. That's just Uncle Cornelius's way of talking," I said. "He's a city lawyer and makes his money gouging people out of their savings." If my uncle could tell stories about Papa, I could tell stories about him. I'd heard both Mama and Papa say it, so it wasn't a lie.

"You're a regular little hothead, aren't you?"

"What if I am?" I glared at Major Dennison, the time for good manners long gone.

The man scowled. "I tell you, boy, sooner or later it's going to come to me where I've seen that chestnut. I never forget a man's face or the shape of a horse. If it turns out you stole him from the Federal Army, I'll see that you go to jail."

With that, Major Dennison strode out of the barn, leading his own swaybacked mare.

I lingered with Ranger and watched the major mount. The way he sat a horse, he didn't deserve a better one, that was for certain. He looked back once and then rode off down the sunlit street.

If the major really did recognize Ranger, I could end up in jail faster than you can say Jack Robinson. Worried in spite of myself, I sat down on an overturned bucket and pondered my future. This might be a good time to begin my journey to Petersburg to find Avery. Rachel was safe, if not happy. No one but her would miss me.

From somewhere outside, I heard my sister singing

"Dixie," most likely in hope of offending someone. Much as I wanted to hop on Ranger's back and leave that very minute, I couldn't go off without telling Rachel good-bye. I decided to wait till dark, being ever watchful as far as the major was concerned.

Before I went back to the house, I cleaned Ranger's saddle. While I was polishing it, I saw something I should have noticed earlier. The captain had branded the leather with his name, "J. K. Powell." I couldn't think of a way to remove those letters. Anything I tried would just draw Major Dennison's attention.

I sighed and threw a blanket over the saddle. I couldn't afford to get rid of it. It was fine leather and well made. I had a long ride ahead of me and would suffer without a good saddle.

"Why do you have to be such a fine specimen?" I asked Ranger. "If you were an ordinary horse, the major would never have noticed you. But no, you have to be as handsome as the king of horses, an animal men remember."

Ranger lowered his head and blew through his nose. He cared nothing about his looks. All he required was a bucket of water and his oats.

◇

Later that afternoon I was back in the stable, hiding from Grandma Colby. She'd been fussing at me all afternoon, and I couldn't bear any more of it.

"Don't sit there snuffling," she'd told me at the lunch table. "Go find a handkerchief and blow your nose. I can't abide rude sounds. That includes slurping your soup."

Turning to Rachel, she'd added, "Remove your elbow from the table at once, young lady. And turn the spoon away from you when you eat soup."

Rachel kicked me under the table and made a face, but she removed the offending elbow.

After lunch I sat down to read one of Uncle Cornelius's translations of Pliny only to have Grandma Colby take the book away. "This is a rare edition," she said sharply. "You'll ruin it with your dirty hands."

When I started to tell her I'd washed them before lunch, she said, "You should be outside exercising. It's bad for a growing boy's health to mope around the house with a book. You'll grow up to be a dreamer like your father."

So I slipped off to the stable to check on Ranger, positive she'd soon follow me there to say I should be inside reading and improving my mind. A few minutes later, I saw Major Dennison rein his horse to a stop just outside the stable door.

The major wasn't alone. Riding behind him was one of the men who'd come to our house with Captain Powell— the skinny runt with the wispy mustache. Hicks, I believe he was called.

The major strode up to me and grabbed the front of my shirt. "I told you I'd remember where I'd seen that horse." Turning to Hicks, he said, "Well, am I right, Corporal?"

Hicks eyed Ranger nervously. At last he said, "He surely does resemble Captain Powell's horse, sir."

·13·

THE MAJOR POINTED at the blanket I'd hung over the saddle. "Go in the stall, Hicks, and see if the captain's name is on that saddle."

Hicks hesitated. "That horse don't like me, sir. Never tolerated nobody but the captain hisself. In fact, I don't see how that puny boy could ever have managed Satan."

Satan. If that wasn't like the captain to name his horse after the devil himself. Truth to tell, Ranger was beginning to show signs of a devilish nature. The whites of his eyes showed and he stamped his feet.

"Do as I say, Corporal Hicks. That's an order!" The major's voice rose.

With great reluctance, Hicks entered the stall. Ranger whinnied and then reared as if he meant to trample the man. I almost hoped he would.

But that cowardly Hicks moved too fast. One big jump backward and he was out of the stall and slamming the door shut. After he slid the bolt home, he turned to the major. "That horse will kill me, sir." His Yankee voice twanged like a bad string on a banjo.

The major swore up a blue streak. Grabbing my arm, he gave me a shake. "Tell me the truth. You stole that horse!"

For the first time Hicks took a good look at me. His eyes

lit with recognition. "Why, he's the one I saw at the house, sir," he said. "His family was sheltering the Bushwhacker we killed."

The major scowled at me. "This means jail for you, boy. And maybe hanging, too. You'll be charged with horse theft for certain and possibly murder, for no one has seen Captain Powell since Hicks and the others left your house."

"Surely the United States Army wouldn't hang a boy." Hicks was clearly shocked by the major's wrathful words.

"Are you contradicting me, Corporal Hicks? Showing disrespect for an officer can result in court-martial."

"Oh, no, sir," Hicks stammered. "No disrespect intended, sir. I was just surprised, sir. I apologize, sir."

The major turned to me. "Go in that stall and fetch me the saddle." So saying, he opened the door and shoved me through.

I landed in a heap at Ranger's feet. For a second I thought the horse might trample me in his rage, but as soon as he saw me, he calmed down. He trusted me—not Hicks.

I longed to jump on his back and ride away, but I knew the major would most likely shoot me. If he shot as badly as he rode, he'd no doubt miss me, but I wasn't brave enough to take the chance. So I picked up the saddle and gave it to the man, certain I was damning myself to jail and maybe hanging.

The major told Hicks to keep his gun on me. Which he did. Slowly the major examined the saddle and then thrust it toward Hicks. "What does that say, Corporal?"

Hicks squinted as if his eyesight was poor. "'J. K. Powell,'" he read. "That's the captain's, all right."

Still holding the saddle, Major Dennison turned to me. "How did you get this horse? And don't feed me any of your lies this time."

"Like I told you last night," I said quickly, "Captain Powell and his men came to our farm looking for James Marshall. They found him upstairs, but he got away. Everyone but the captain rode off after him." I paused to swallow. It was hard to keep from shaking.

"That's right," Hicks said, almost as if he were encouraging me. "The captain stayed in the house."

"Well, he shoved us all in a room and locked the door and then he went after his men." My words sounded weak and foolish, but I kept on talking, praying the major would believe me. "I don't know what happened to the captain, sir. But we climbed out a window and hid down in a gully. We were scared. Didn't know what they'd do to us when they came back."

I paused to take a breath. My throat and mouth had dried up, and I would have given a lot for a drink of water.

Major Dennison scowled down at me. "Go on," he said,

"Powell's men killed James Marshall and brought him back to our house," I went on. "They hanged his corpse from a tree limb and burned our house down. Drank all Papa's liquor while they were at it and left at dawn." I scowled at Hicks, hating him and Dennison and all the other Yankees.

"We rode all over, searching for the captain," Hicks put in. "Not a hide nor hair of him did we see. It was like he'd been carried off by the devil hisself. Least that's what we thought."

In my opinion, every single Yankee deserved to be carried off by the devil, Captain Powell having first priority and the major second.

Major Dennison ignored Hicks and focused on me. "And the horse?"

"I came across him a few days later down by the river, wet and shivering, like he'd fallen in or something." I glanced at Ranger, glad he couldn't speak up and tell the truth. "Our mother had died of fever, and I thought my sister and I could ride him to Grandma Colby's house. I found the horse, you see. That's not the same as stealing him."

"I'd say there's a mighty fine line between stealing and finding," the major said. "Especially considering you lied to me and claimed he was a birthday present. You know full well you should have turned him over to me this morning."

Full of wrath, the major turned to Hicks. "Tie the boy's wrists and take him down to the jailhouse, Corporal. I'm not certain I believe a word of his story. If he lied to me once, he'd do it again."

Hicks opened his mouth as if to protest but shut it at the sight of the major's angry face. "Yes, sir," he mumbled.

I put up a fight to keep from being arrested, but it did me no good. The major gave my head a cuff so hard it half dazed me. After that, Hicks didn't have much trouble tying me. Lord, was he inept. If I'd been left alone, I could have wiggled out of those knots in no time.

But I had no opportunity to try. The major picked me up and slung me over the back of the corporal's old nag as if I were a sack of grain bound for the mill. Or a dead man. He handed Hicks the reins and took Ranger's bridle. The horse reared again, and kicked the major in the leg. Howling a string of curses, the man took to beating the horse into submission. It made me cry, for Ranger was the finest horse I'd ever known and he didn't deserve to be treated so badly.

Though Major Dennison didn't have an easy time of it, he managed to lead Ranger behind his own horse. Hicks followed, keeping a safe distance between his horse and Ranger, who danced about and tossed his head.

As we passed the house, Rachel came running out, followed by the aunts and Uncle Cornelius. Grandma Colby walked as far as the edge of the porch. While the others asked where the major was taking me and why, my grandmother stood silently, hand pressed to her heart, as if she were about to die of disgrace. It was strange to see them from my position. A family turned upside down.

"Your nephew is a criminal, sir," Major Dennison told my uncle. "A horse thief and most likely a murderer. It's my duty to arrest him and see he is sent to jail to await a fair trial."

"But the boy's only thirteen years old," Aunt Esther protested.

"And an orphan as well," added Aunt Hester.

"Haswell could not have murdered anyone," Aunt Esther said. "He's a good boy."

"A little foolish sometimes," Aunt Hester put in, "but nonetheless a good boy."

"As for the horse, it must be a mistake," Aunt Esther said.

"No Colby has ever stolen anything," Aunt Hester insisted.

"It's not in the blood," Aunt Esther agreed.

Suddenly, Rachel threw herself at the major, pummeling his legs and the horse's sides. If the nag had had any spirit, he would have reared up and kicked Rachel, but he took his drubbing as if it were no more than fly bites. "Let Haswell go, you dirty Yankee! Let him go!" my sister cried.

While Ranger reared and pawed the air behind him, the

major raised his whip and slashed the air a half inch from Rachel's head. If he'd struck her, he would have cut her face open.

Rachel stepped back, fists clenched, face scarlet, breathing hard. "Let my brother go! He didn't steal that horse and he didn't kill anybody! It was Mama who—" Rachel covered her mouth with both hands and silenced herself. "Let him go!"

At this point Uncle Cornelius finally spoke up. "Come now, Thomas, there's no need to take the boy to jail. I'm certain this is all a misunderstanding." He paused and studied the major's wrathful face. Gesturing at Ranger, he added, "You're welcome to the horse, but leave Haswell here. I'll take full responsibility for him."

Major Dennison considered this proposal. "I must say I've found you to be a most hospitable and generous host, Cornelius. But this boy has committed a serious crime. I dare not leave him with you." Turning to Hicks, he said, "Let's go."

The aunts and Rachel rushed to my side as if they feared they'd never see me again. Rachel grabbed hold of my arms and pulled till I cried out in pain. Grandma Colby stayed on the porch, as speechless as if she'd turned to stone.

"Hicks! Get a move on!" Major Dennison shouted.

"Yes, sir." Despite my family's protests, Hicks rode on behind the major, taking care to keep a good distance.

By the time we got to the Winchester city jail, I was dizzy from hanging across that horse's back. In fact, when Hicks lifted me off, I almost swooned. If he hadn't caught me, I'd have fallen flat on my face. I guessed the blood had all rushed to my head.

"You all right?" Hicks asked.

"'Course I am!" I tried to speak up, but my voice sounded a bit puny. And I wobbled when I walked. Hicks kept a hand on my shoulder. I reckoned he was thinking I'd run off. Believe me, I would have if I'd had the strength.

After leaving a soldier to deal with the horses, Major Dennison led the way, favoring the leg Ranger had kicked. Despite my circumstances, that pleased me.

While the major explained the situation to the prison guard, Hicks held my arm in a loose grip. By now I was feeling strong enough to pull away, but I feared I'd be shot if I made a move. So I stood beside Hicks and waited to hear my fate.

"He'll be put on trial," the guard said, "when the judge has time. Meanwhile, I'll lock him up."

Hicks handed me over to the guard. "He's just a boy," he told the guard in a low voice. "Go easy on him."

The guard nodded and led me down a dark corridor lined with locked doors made of bars. Unlocking one, he gave me a little push. "Go on in, boy. It ain't so bad. You ought to see Anderson Prison. Makes this seem like heaven."

He locked the door behind me, and I sat down in a corner. The floor was earth, covered with moldy straw. A blanket and a bucket for waste were the only other things in the cell. On one wall there was a little barred window too high up to see out of. That was it. That and the smell of sweat and urine and dirt and old misery. The cell wasn't big enough to stretch your arms out. And I was just a boy, small for my age.

I'd seen the jail from the outside many times. Papa and Mama, Rachel and Avery and I had walked past it frequently when we visited Uncle Cornelius in the old days before the war. As Papa used to say, an evening stroll was a good way to escape Uncle Cornelius and his after-supper rants about politics and such. I'd often wondered what the jail was like inside, but I'd never dreamed I'd find out one day.

I remembered Rachel asking Papa about it. She was four or five years old, and already smart as she could be.

"Why, that's the jail, Rachel," Papa had said.

"What's a jail?" she'd asked, seeking to enlarge her vocabulary.

"It's where people go who have committed a crime," Papa answered.

"Bad people," I added, thinking to scare Rachel.

She'd looked at me, her face serious. "Then I expect that's where you'll go, Haswell."

Papa had laughed. "'Out of the mouths of babes,'" he'd said. "Be warned, son, and behave yourself."

Rachel the prophet. I hadn't thought it funny then. And I certainly didn't find it funny now.

The day passed. Sometimes I was bored half to death, but mostly I worried about being hanged. Surely Hicks was right. The Union Army wouldn't hang a boy. But then I'd remember Major Dennison's red face and angry eyes. Oh, he'd hang me if he were the judge, I was certain of it. Well, all I could do was hope the judge was not the same sort of vengeful man.

Around dusk a guard brought me something resembling hash in a tin bowl. Supper, he said. Coffee came with it. At least I supposed that's what it was. Black and nasty was how it tasted. As for the hash, I downed it because my belly was empty and needed filling. And it took my mind off hanging, for a while at least.

Slowly the little bit of sky I could see darkened to black. And so did the cell. Things rustled in the straw, and soon

I was scratching bug bites. A mouse or a rat chittered nearby. I curled up small as I could in the smelly blanket and tried to sleep, but thoughts of the gallows tree kept creeping into my mind. I'd never seen a hanging, but I'd heard about them. What was it like to climb up to that platform under the gallows tree and look out at the crowd waiting to watch you die? To know you had just a few more minutes to breathe and see the sky? Would they blindfold me? How would the rope feel around my neck? Would I cry and beg, would I struggle, or would I just stand there and feel the platform drop open beneath my feet? How long would I live? Would it hurt? Would Mama and Papa be waiting for me across Jordan?

While I lay there tormenting myself with questions I couldn't answer, I heard footsteps. Someone was walking toward my cell. In the dark I made out the figure of a soldier. Slowly and quietly he unlocked the door and stood over me.

My first thought was he had come to take me to the hanging tree. I started to cry out, but his hand covered my mouth.

"Hush," he whispered. "It's me, Otis Hicks. Don't make a sound."

·14·

WHEN HE TOOK HIS HAND AWAY, I began to shiver. "Am I to be hanged now?"

"Is that what you think?" Hicks squatted beside me. "Trust me, boy, I've come to get you out of this place."

"Get me out?" I couldn't understand his meaning. Was he trying to help me? Why would he do that? He'd be risking his own life.

Hicks pulled me to my feet, hushing me all the while. From down the hall I heard loud laughter and voices.

"I stole whiskey for the guards," Hicks whispered. "And set up a poker game. Took the keys when they was too drunk to notice."

Even though I'd figured out his meaning, I still didn't know why he was helping me escape. "Why are you—"

"Not now," he whispered. "Come on, will you?"

I followed him out of the cell. Edging along the corridor as quietly as we could, we got past the guards while they argued over the fine rules of poker. Hicks shoved me outside the building just as one of the men yelled, "Hey, Hicks, ain't you playing another hand?"

"You boys are just too smart for me," he called back. "You cleaned out my pockets, for sure."

They laughed and went back to playing. I turned to Hicks and asked again, "Why are you—"

"Hush." He pulled me along, sticking close to the jail wall, where the shadows were blackest. When we came in sight of the stable, he stopped. "You want that cussed horse, right?"

I studied his long face in the moonlight. "Is this a trick to get me hanged for certain?"

Hicks shook his head. "Don't be so damn dumb. I got it all worked out. Just go along with what I say and we'll be on our way."

With that, he grabbed my shoulder and strolled downhill to the army stable. Two guards lounged by the doors, smoking pipes. They looked up when they saw us. "Hey, Otis, what's your pleasure?" one called.

Hicks smiled. "Boys, remember that horse Major Dennison brought in this afternoon, the one that used to belong to Captain Powell? Name's Satan. Big fine chestnut."

"Hoo, boy!" one said. "You think anybody could forget *that* devil?"

"Why, he just about destroyed the stall we put him in."

Otis laughed. "Well, ain't I the lucky fellow? The major sent me to fetch him."

"What does the major want with a horse at midnight?" the guard asked.

Hicks laughed again, a little louder this time. "You know how the major is once he gets a notion." He leaned a little closer to the guard and added conspiratorially, "Especially if he's drinking or gambling. Why, there's no telling what that there man will want. And Lord help you if he don't get it."

The guard spat in the dirt. "Ain't that the truth?"

"Hey," the other guard said. "Isn't that the very boy the major put in jail for stealing the horse?"

"Why, Charlie, he is in fact the very same boy." Hicks gave me a little shake to show he had a good grip on me. "The major asked me to get him out of jail because he's the only one can handle Satan. Didn't I tell you the man's been at the bottle? Him and the boy's uncle, both. They got some sort of bet going."

Charlie turned to his companion. "What do you think, Caleb?"

Caleb shrugged. "Don't make no matter to me where the boy goes. Or the horse, either. Good riddance to both of 'em, I say. And you, too, for that matter." He winked to show he was jesting with Hicks.

"Go on and get the plagued animal, then." Charlie laughed. "It's your hide, not mine."

Hicks let me into the stable. When we found Ranger's stall, the horse reared up and whinnied. His hooves struck the boards with a sound like thunder. Hicks took a few step backward.

"Seems like he's in a right foul temper," he muttered. "You sure you can manage that animal?"

Instead of answering Hicks, I went right up to Ranger and spoke nice and calm to him, telling him what a fine steed he was and stroking his head where his coat felt like cropped velvet. His nostrils flared and he stamped his feet, but gradually he composed himself and let me saddle him. By the time he was ready to go, Ranger was nuzzling my face and neck, breathing his warm horsy breath down the front of my shirt. It seemed he was as glad to see me as I was to see him.

I brought Ranger out of his stall, admiring the grace of his walk and the curve of his neck. Hicks kept a respectful distance.

"You lead the horse," he said. "I'll walk ahead."

The guards watched us come out of the stable. Ranger acted skittish, but he let me lead him.

"Think you can manage?" Caleb asked Hicks. "Not that I'm volunteering to go along and help you."

Charlie laughed and slapped his thigh. "You'd be more of a hindrance than a help."

"I'll be all right as long as the boy leads him," Hicks admitted.

"Be sure and bring the little Rebel back," Caleb said. "There'll be hell to pay if he gets away. To hear the major talk, you'd think that there boy was Mosby hisself."

Once we were out of sight of the stables, I mounted Ranger. With Hicks walking beside me, I led the way down side streets and alleys, doing my best to avoid encountering a guard on patrol. Every now and then we saw soldiers and hid in the shadows till they passed. Luckily for us, most of them were coming back from the taverns, too full of merriment to notice us. But one group lingered just ahead, blocking our path, laughing and talking. To avoid trouble, Hicks and I cut down an alley and waited for them to be on their way.

"Where are you heading?" Hicks whispered.

"My uncle's house. I have to get a few things." Mainly what I wanted was Papa's revolver and the ammunition hidden under my mattress. That and some food from the pantry. If I had time, I'd write a note to Rachel. I didn't dare wake her to say good-bye. She'd cry and beg to go with me. Rouse the whole house. And I'd be back in the major's hands without hope of another escape.

"And then what?" Hicks asked.

"My brother's in Petersburg. I'm going down there and do my best to find him." Never had I missed Avery so much, never had I wanted to see him so badly. He'd know what to do. Things would be all right again if I could just find him.

The soldiers began moving on, their voices fading as they walked past. I was about to leave the alley, but Hicks had more to say.

"There's a siege around Petersburg. You know that?"

"Of course I know that. Everybody knows that."

"The Union's got the town surrounded as tight as a noose around a dead man's neck. Nobody gets in, nobody gets out."

I scowled at him, angered by his cowardly opinions. "Don't worry about me. I'm not scared of you Yankees. I'll find my brother."

Hicks gave me a mournful look. "It ain't going to be easy."

"Why do you care?" I felt my temper rise. "I wouldn't be here right now if you and your cronies hadn't come to our farm looking for James Marshall. My mother got sick and died on account of what you did. Rachel and I haven't got a home because you burned it down. Thanks to you and this war, we haven't got crops to plant or livestock or anything!"

The words spewed out of me like vomit. I hated the Yankees so much I thought I'd rather have been hanged than be beholden to Hicks. "I hope you and Captain Powell and all you Yankees burn in hellfire!"

I was about to gallop away, but Hicks reached out and grabbed the bridle. "Hold on, Haswell," he begged. "I'm sorry for what I done at your house. Sorry for lots of other things I done in this war. It's why I got you out of jail. To try to make up for all that—and to tell you how bad I feel."

"You think apologizing is going to make everything right again? You think it'll bring Mama back? Or our farm?" It seemed there was more sorrow and anger crammed into me than my heart could hold. I felt it pushing its way up my throat till I thought I'd choke on it. "I hope you feel bad all your life. I hope you go to your grave feeling bad. I hope you burn in hell feeling bad!"

Hicks stepped back and stared at me as if I'd put a curse on him. Maybe I had. But he deserved it. They all deserved it.

"You don't mean that, Haswell," he said. "Surely you don't."

"I mean every word of it!" I saw tears glitter in his eyes, but I didn't care. "And more!"

"But, Haswell, it weren't my fault. I tried to stop them other boys from burning the house. Honest I did. And it weren't me who shot that Bushwhacker. Or hurt your mama."

I clenched my teeth and glared down at the man. He was a sorry sight, but he wasn't worthy of my pity. Or my forgiveness.

"God Almighty, boy, haven't both of us seen enough of war and dying and misery?" Hicks looked me straight in the eyes as he spoke. "It ain't just the South that's suffering. You got to know that. It's all of us."

He was speaking from his heart, but even though his honesty shamed me, I couldn't forgive him for what he'd done. I sat on Ranger's back and stared down at him, my eyes cold.

"I done what I was told, Haswell," Hicks said. "That's what soldiers do. Obey their officers."

Hicks started coughing then. Like many another soldier I'd seen, he was worn down before his time, old and wasted, though he couldn't have been more than twenty. The cough was a bad one, deep in his chest and hard enough to make tears run down his face. I'd heard James Marshall cough that way, and I wondered if Avery was also afflicted.

"What are you going to do?" I asked. "If you go back to camp, the major will most likely have you hanged in my place."

Hicks scratched his head. Lice, most likely. My own scalp was itching already. Seemed the varmints were everywhere. You just couldn't get rid of them.

Stifling another cough, Hicks said, "Home. I'm going home to Pennsylvania."

"But the war's not over."

Otis Hicks shrugged. "It will be soon enough. General Sheridan's got orders to take us down to Petersburg. I ain't got the stomach for no more fighting."

"You can be hanged for deserting," I said.

"I know it." He started walking away but turned and looked back, his weary face ghostly in the moonlight. "You be careful, Haswell. The way you're going, you might find yourself smack in the middle of a battle."

I sat on Ranger and watched him begin his long journey home. His back was bent and he favored one leg. I still hated the man for what he'd done to us, but at the same time I was grateful to him for saving my life. Maybe in his eyes the two things balanced each other out somehow. When he was almost out of earshot, I called after him. "Hey! Thanks for getting me out of jail."

Otis Hicks raised a hand in farewell and continued on his way.

When I could see him no longer, I signaled Ranger to move on. Despite all Hicks had done to grieve me, I found myself hoping he'd make it back to Pennsylvania.

·15·

Ever watchful for soldiers, I approached my uncle's house and tied Ranger to a tall oak tree where the shadows were darkest.

"Stay," I whispered, "and don't make a sound."

Light shone from the parlor window. I crept close and peered inside. Uncle Cornelius and Major Dennison were deep in the whiskey and talking loud enough to be heard outside.

"Look here, Corny, you've got no defense left in the Valley," Major Dennison was saying. "Jubal Early's troops are all dead, captured, or running for their lives. Mosby's holed up somewhere, but he can't do much harm anymore. And Sheridan's about to head for Petersburg. Once he arrives, he'll end the siege and the Confederacy will collapse."

"Oh, now," rumbled my uncle, "it's not over yet. No, sir. Petersburg's secure. You Federals have been trying to defeat our men since last summer, and where's it gotten you?"

The major laughed again. "You Southern boys just won't quit till you're all dead." He broke off to take a swallow of whiskey.

"Ah, what's the sense of talking about it?" Uncle Cornelius sounded weary. "Seems there's many a dead man on both sides. Maybe it would be better to see it end." He rose from the chair with some effort and yawned. "Time to call it a night."

Major Dennison yawned, too. Tossing down the last of his whiskey, he stood up. "I'll be on my way home soon. Just in time, too. Couldn't bear another summer here. Don't know how you stand it. Too damn hot."

Uncle Cornelius blew out the lamps, and the two of them vanished into the dark hall.

I stayed where I was to give them time to settle down. After twenty minutes or so, I climbed the old fir tree at the side of the porch. I'd heard John tell Avery that's how he sneaked in and out of the house. It was just as easy as he'd claimed. Like climbing a ladder.

I stepped onto the porch roof and slowly slid my bedroom window up. Safe inside, I removed the revolver and the ammunition from their hiding place. I lit a candle and found paper and pencil on John's desk. It seemed nothing in his room had changed since he'd joined the army. His books, paper, pencils, and pens waited for him to come home.

Dere Rachel, I wrote. *You won't belive this but Otis Hicks set me free from jail and tricked the gards into giving me Ranger. Now he has deserted and is going home to Pensilvany. I hope he gets there for he isn't relly a bad man even tho he's a Yankee and has done rongful deeds.*

I paused and thought about what to say next. *Don't be mad at me for going without you. I have to find Avery as fast as I can so he can take care of us and the farm. We will come to Winchester and get you. Wait for us. Your brother, Haswell C. Magruder.*

I spent some time signing my name with fancy flourishes. Next I folded James Marshall's letter in with Rachel's and added a P.S.:

Please mail this to James Marshall's father so he'll know he's dead. Please tell him ware he's buryed and how he died. Shot in the chest not the back. I woud do it but you spell and rite better than I do.

I tiptoed across the hall to Rachel's room and slowly pushed the door open. At her bedside I stood over her for a few seconds and watched her sleep. Her hair was loose and spread on the pillow. She had Sophia in her arms, but her face looked pale and sad. I'd never noticed how much she resembled Mama.

I wanted to kiss her good-bye, but I was scared of waking her. Instead, I tucked the letters under the doll and left my sister to her dreams. I hoped they were good ones.

Making no more noise than a cat, I crept down the back stairs and sneaked into the pantry. I filled a kerchief with apples, cheese, biscuits, and cold ham. Tying it into a bundle, I slipped out the door and headed for the stable to get feed for Ranger.

The stars were out and the moon was sinking down from heaven toward earth. A cool wind stirred the tree branches, bringing with it a nice damp smell, the kind that comes when the ground's warming up and things are starting to grow. It was March, and I could almost smell plants bursting out of the earth and reaching for light.

I touched Papa's revolver to make certain it was still in my pocket and ran to the oak tree. Ranger was waiting quietly, just as I'd told him to. I climbed onto his back and set out to find my brother.

◊

I rode through the night, sometimes falling asleep in the saddle, trying hard to put as many miles as I could between Winchester and me. By dawn Ranger was showing signs of fatigue. I reckoned we still had almost two hundred miles to go. At this rate it would take at least three weeks to get to Petersburg—probably more if I ran into trouble along the way.

I checked the road behind me. No one was coming. Up ahead I heard nothing except birds singing in the woods. Ranger and I might have been the last survivors of the war.

I saw a stream flowing out of the woods and followed it into the trees. When I was sure we were out of sight of passersby on the road, I slipped from the saddle, as worn and weary as I'd ever been. Ranger nuzzled me, and I reached into the saddlebags for his oats. While he ate his breakfast, I ate mine—half a biscuit and a piece of ham. Though it didn't fill my belly, I didn't dare eat more. My food had to last as long as possible. We both drank deeply from the stream. No danger of using up the water.

By then the sun was already high in the sky and the day showed signs of being warm and fair. I bedded down in my blankets and fell asleep at once, one hand gripping the revolver, just in case.

We passed several days like that, traveling by night and sleeping by day. When I was little I was scared of the dark. I'd lie awake long after everyone was asleep, listening to the stairs creak, sure the bogeyman Grandma Colby told me about was coming to get me on account of all the bad things I'd done. No matter how hard a paddling I got, I'd wet the bed rather than face the outhouse in the nighttime. Going there was bad enough in daylight, when I could see the spiders and their webs. And there was always the chance a monster of some sort lived down in the pit, waiting to grab me.

Now, of course, I knew Grandma Colby made up the bogeyman to scare me into behaving. And I knew the only thing in the outhouse pit was what we put there ourselves. But still, when I rode along those dark roads with no company but Ranger, my imagination turned every sound into danger. Rustling noises meant Yankees were nearby. A twig snapping meant a half-crazy deserter was sneaking up to kill me and steal Ranger. The wind sighing through the trees was the whisper of dead soldiers longing to come back and finish their lives. The hoot of an owl reminded me of Grandma Colby's belief that the owl was death's messenger: he called to warn you your time on earth was nearly up. So far I reckoned the owl had been calling someone else, not me. But sooner or later my turn would come.

I swear I shivered and shook the whole night long. There were times I actually wished I'd brought Rachel with me. Her chattering would've been easier to listen to than those noises in the dark. Nothing cheered me more than the gray dawn slowly lighting the world, bringing back its colors and shapes.

As soon as the sun was fully up, I'd lead Ranger off the road and deep into the woods. We'd eat a little of what we had and bed down to sleep. Sometimes I saw parties of soldiers on the road. I reckoned they were Sheridan's men, heading for Petersburg. Their uniforms were too good to be Confederates. One night I passed so close to a Yankee camp I heard their voices round the fire. I paused to listen, for I hadn't had human company for a long while.

A soldier was singing "Tenting on the Old Camp Ground" while another played along on the harmonica.

Someone plinked a banjo. It was enough to make you cry to hear the sad words of the song come floating through the darkness.

> *Many are the hearts that are weary tonight,*
> *Wishing for the war to cease;*
> *Many are the hearts looking for the right*
> *To see the dawn of peace.*
> *Dying tonight,*
> *Dying tonight,*
> *Dying on the old camp ground.*

For once I wasn't ashamed to give in to my sorrow. All alone on the road, I mourned Mama and Papa and James Marshall and my home. My heart was weary, I wished the war were over, I wished no one would die tonight or any other night.

There was silence for a few moments and then a soldier shouted, "Why, boys, let's not put on more agony than we already have." He must have had a concertina for he commenced to play and sing a lively song about the Cumberland Gap.

As the Yankees' voices rose, I rode away into the night. Truthfully, I would have liked to walk into the firelight and sit down amongst those soldiers and feel the warmth of their bodies. At that moment I was so lonesome I didn't care which side they were on.

· 16 ·

AFTER A WEEK OR SO of nocturnal traveling, I figured Ranger and I were beyond Yankee-held towns. So one morning we just kept going.

In the daylight I got a better picture of the land. I passed fields and houses and barns, burned or shot to pieces by cannonballs. Most of the farms were deserted, but once in a while I saw families living in the ruins of their houses. They were as ragged as I was. Children watched me pass, their eyes full of fear and worry. No one raised a hand in greeting. Even the dogs cowered and ran at the sight of me. They were too beaten down to bark.

It was strange to see trees showing the first faint greens and pinks of spring. It seemed everything should be as dead as the salt-sown fields of Carthage after the Punic Wars. Papa had told me the Romans wanted Carthage obliterated, never to thrive again, never to be a threat to the Empire, so they'd done what they could to kill everything, even the land itself. I hoped the Yankees weren't hoping to destroy us completely and utterly and for all eternity.

It cheered me to see dandelions blooming in the weeds. Overhead, birds sang as if nothing had changed. I guessed in their world nothing had. Spring had come. It was time to build nests and find mates and raise families. Just like always.

Days passed, one pretty much the same as another, except sometimes it rained and sometimes it didn't. The biscuits got damp, and I had to pick out the weevils before I ate. I must confess I was too tired to bother sometimes. Papa told Mama once that the weevils she found in the flour were most likely good for us. He'd studied about tribes in faraway places that ate all sorts of insects and grubs and such. Though Mama scoffed at the very notion, Papa must have been right because I didn't throw up my food. But I didn't develop a fondness for it. And I certainly didn't grow fat on it.

Worse yet, I wasn't always sure where I was. The countryside looked different from the way I remembered it on trips with my father. Some towns were burned and deserted. Familiar landmarks—a church on a hilltop or an old mill, were in ruins, almost unrecognizable. Signposts were missing or turned the wrong way.

One day I followed a trail across open ground and found myself in a soldiers' burial ground. It was almost dusk. Wooden grave markers leaned this way and that, as weather-worn as if they were centuries old. Suddenly, Ranger stumbled on something. I looked down and saw a skull leering up at me. A glance around showed me more skulls and bones. It seemed the soldiers had been buried hastily in shallow graves. The rain and snow had washed the earth away, and there they were, hundreds of skeletons rising from their graves. Some still wore the remains of their uniforms.

Ranger shied and pawed the earth. He didn't like the

place any more than I did. As I urged him on, I heard someone laugh. Ranger froze and so did I. A skeletal figure loomed up from the evening mist rolling across the field. I knew who it was. Death. The owl had finally called my name.

"Hey, boy, don't be afeared!" the figure called. "They's dead men all over, but they can't hurt you or each other no more. All killed in the fighting last fall. Dead as dead can be. Whether they likes it or not."

Still frozen, I watched the man come closer. He had two dead muskrats in one hand and a trap in the other. His wild gray beard hung down to his waist. His slouch hat hid much of his face. The clothes he wore were held together with patches.

"I don't aim to hurt you, boy." He held up the muskrats. "Thought you might be hungry."

My stomach rumbled at the thought of muskrat stew.

The old man laughed again. "I thought so! The belly don't lie, now, do it?"

When he took hold of Ranger's reins, I reached for my pistol. Finding my voice at last, I said, "Let my horse go!"

The old man did as I asked. "Pardon me, boy. I was just a-trying to lead you home. Thought you might share supper with me and my wife. We got us a cabin up the hill."

My head warred with my stomach. I wanted food so bad. A warm place. People to talk to. But what if the old man aimed to rob me? Or kill me?

"I mean you no harm," the old man insisted. "I'm Isaac Caples. Why, if you lived in these parts, you'd most likely be kin to me."

"I'm Haswell Colby Magruder and I'm a long way from

home and I'm no kin of yours." But I didn't pull the trigger and I didn't ride away. It was almost full dark and the wind had begun to blow colder. And I had no idea where I was.

"Where you from and where you bound?" Mr. Caples asked.

"I'm from Winchester," I said, "heading for Petersburg."

He shook his head. "You've gone a sight too far south. Come along home with me and fill your belly. Get yourself some sleep. Tomorrow I'll point you in the right direction."

Too tired and hungry to do anything else, I followed Mr. Caples across the burial ground. Behind me, I heard the dead men's bones whispering in the wind, begging us to take them back to firelight and muskrat stew and soft, warm beds.

I saw the light shining through the trees before I saw the cabin. An old woman holding a lantern stood in the doorway. Her hair was white and pulled into a tight knot on the back of her head.

"Isaac," she called. "Who's that with you?"

As we stepped into the light of the old woman's lantern, Mr. Caples said, "This here's Mr. Haswell Colby Magruder. He's not from these parts, so he's no kin of ours, but he's heading for Petersburg."

"Why's he want to go there?" the old woman asked. "There's no food in Petersburg."

"I never did ask the boy why he's going there." Mr. Caples turned to me. "Why do you want to go to Petersburg? They been under a siege since last summer."

"My brother Avery's there with the army, and I aim to find him and bring him home."

"Yankee or Confederate army?" Mr. Caples asked.

"Why, Confederate!"

"Now, now, don't get all riled up," Mr. Caples said. "I was just asking."

The old woman came to my side. "I'm Mrs. Annie Caples. My husband never did have no manners. You come inside and rest yourself while I cook up them muskrats. Isaac will tend to your horse."

Her voice was soft and kind. I slid off Ranger and let Mr. Caples lead him around back. Once inside the cabin, I lay down by the fire and fell fast asleep.

It must have been the smell of muskrat stew that finally woke me. Mrs. Caples had fixed a big bowl for me, along with a chunk of bread and a mug of apple cider. It was the best meal I'd eaten in a long time. It was also the first time my belly had been full since I'd left Winchester.

While I ate, the Capleses told me stories about the war. Two of their sons had died in the terrible fighting at Cold Harbor. Another son had died of typhus in Richmond. His widow lived nearby, and she was so out of her head with grief she could scarcely care for her five children. Nobody had enough to eat. Like everyone else, they were weary of the war.

"We saw our sons off to war in 1861," Mr. Caples said. "All three rode with Jubal Early. Lord Almighty, we were so proud of those boys. They looked grand in their uniforms, clean and scrubbed and rosy-faced."

Mrs. Caples blew her nose. "How I wish I'd kept them home," she said. "But we all thought they'd run the Yankees out of Virginia and be home for Christmas. We had no idea what lay ahead."

"Nor did they," Mr. Caples said. "Nor did they, poor boys."

"Thomas and James came home that first winter." Mrs. Caples sighed and blew her nose again. "We hardly knew them. Their fine uniforms were in rags, their faces thin, their eyes full of shadows."

"Annie here tried to keep them from going back, but they went anyway. Stubborn as mules, them boys. From the time they were babes they done what they wanted."

Mrs. Caples reached out and grasped Mr. Caples's hand, "Never saw any of our boys again. All three gone."

The cabin grew silent. Sparks shot up the chimney. The candle flame leaned to the side. Wax ran down and puddled on the table.

"They didn't ride back to Jubal Early the way they done the first time," Mr. Caples said. "They didn't look like heroes no more. I reckon it's hard to think noble thoughts when men are screaming and dying all around you."

Long after I lay down on my pallet by the fire I thought about what Mr. Caples had said. I guessed he was wiser than I'd thought at first. And a deal more trustworthy.

❖

The next morning Mr. and Mrs. Caples fed me fried bread and apple cider. After I ate all I could, they gave me a new supply of provisions for myself and Ranger. Mr. Caples drew me a map showing me the best way to Petersburg and told me where to watch for Yankee soldiers.

"You be careful now, young Haswell," Mr. Caples said. "You've still got at least a week's journey ahead of you."

"Yes, sir," I said. "And thank you for all you've done for me. I'm sorry I mistook you for a villain."

Mr. Caples laughed. "Well, now, I reckon some folks have called me a villain, but they was no-'count Yankees." He slapped Ranger on his hindquarters. "Be on your way now. Come back and visit some day. I reckon we'll be here till we get called up yonder to see our boys."

Although I knew full well I had to leave, I would have enjoyed staying with the Capleses a while longer. They put me in mind of my Magruder grandparents, warm and welcoming and kind.

· 17 ·

Not long after I left the Capleses' cabin, rain began to fall. It came down hard and steady, as if it never meant to quit. The road dissolved into thick red mud, channeled with streams and puddles of water. The mud sucked at Ranger's hooves, making every step difficult. He plodded along as if he were pulling a plow.

Soon my head began to ache, then my chest, my arms, my legs. I got so light-headed I could scarcely sit up straight. I shook with cold and burned with heat. More than anything, I wanted to throw myself down in the weeds and lie there till I died. But sick as I knew myself to be, I kept going, watching for a house with lights in the window. If I were lucky, I'd find someone to help me like Mama helped James Marshall.

In the evening of the third day, I saw a cabin set way back from the road with light shining from a window. It was nearly dark and the rain was still falling, but I could make out a thin plume of gray smoke rising from the chimney, barely discernible against the heavy clouds.

Praying the inhabitants would be as kindly as the Capleses, I turned Ranger down the lane leading to the cabin. The water was up to the horse's hocks, but he lurched along, with me clutching the reins. My hands shook, my teeth chattered, my head felt two or three times its usual size. I was thinking this was my last chance. If the folks who lived here turned me away, I wouldn't last the night.

When I got closer, a pack of dogs started barking. Ranger hesitated. I saw they were fenced in and urged the horse on.

A boy peered out of the window and shouted to someone behind him, "Polly, it's a boy on a horse. Should I let the dogs loose?"

Another face appeared, a girl's this time. She took one look at me and vanished. A few seconds later, the cabin door opened and she stepped out onto the porch.

"What do you want?" she called. In her hands was a musket old enough to have belonged to her great granddaddy. The way she held it told me she knew how to use it. And her eyes told me she'd pull the trigger if she had to.

I urged Ranger toward the cabin anyway. By now I was swaying from one side to the other. I couldn't stay in the saddle much longer.

"Please," I croaked, "I'm half dead of fever." I reached out and felt myself plunge into blackness.

The next thing I knew, I was lying on a pallet made of blankets and quilts. The fire was burning bright, warming me through and through. My clothes were hanging on the back of a chair, drying. Under the blankets I was naked.

I turned my head and look around. The girl, Polly, was watching me. When she saw my eyes open, she hopped up and offered me a tin cup full of hot broth. "Sip it slow," she warned me. "You don't want to throw it up. Be a waste of good food if you done that."

"Thanks." I held the cup, but my hands shook so bad

the broth slopped over the sides. Polly reached out and steadied the cup and helped me drink.

"You feeling any better?" she asked.

I nodded. "Warm, dry, out of the rain."

"It took me and Henry both to drag you inside. You slept so long I was afeared you was dead." She paused and her thin face flushed. "Hope you don't mind us taking off your clothes. We had to get you dry."

"Where's my revolver?" I asked. "And my horse?"

Polly picked up the gun and handed it to me. "Don't worry. We ain't thieves. Henry put your horse in a shed behind the cabin, so he ain't out in the rain. He's a mighty fine animal."

"Those dogs won't bother him, will they?"

"No, they're just old coon dogs. I never knowed them to bite anybody. They just bark and growl and look real mean. Scaring people off, that's what they're good for."

I sipped some more broth. It was almost as good as Mama's, and it slid down my throat in a comforting way.

"I'm Polly O'Brien. What's your name, and how come you're in these parts?" Polly asked.

"Haswell Magruder. I'm heading to Petersburg to find my brother, Avery. He's there with the Confederates, holding off the Yankees."

"Do your ma and pa know where you are?" Polly asked. "Or did you just run off?"

I turned my head to the fire so she wouldn't see the tears in my eyes. Being sick has a way of making a person cry. It must weaken you or something. "Mama and Papa are dead," I said. "My sister and I need to find Avery and bring him home, so we can keep our farm going."

Polly didn't say anything for a while. "Our ma's dead,

too," she finally said. "Fever took her a couple of years ago. And Pa's at the war. We ain't heard from him in a long time, so could be he's dead, too. Henry and me been doing our best, but we ain't had much luck. Except we're still alive. Some might say that's lucky."

While she talked, I studied her face. Freckles on top of freckles, more than a person could count. Greeny gray eyes, a wild mop of red hair, a straight little nose. She reminded me of Maura, our Irish maid, the one who ran off with the Yankee soldier. Pretty. But sad. Especially her eyes.

"I hear the war's almost over," I said.

"So they say. I hope it's true."

"Me, too."

We fell silent again. The fire was burning low, and shadows hid most of Polly's face.

"How old are you?" I asked.

"Almost fifteen."

"I'm thirteen."

"Henry's only eleven, but he thinks he's all growed up. The war, I reckon. It ages a person, don't you think?" She smiled at me. "You want some more broth? Or water?"

I shook my head. "I just want to sleep."

Polly got to her feet. "Henry and me sleep in the loft. He's up there now. If you want anything, just holler." She smiled again, showing a little dimple in one cheek. "That is, if you got the voice to holler."

"Don't worry. I'll be fine."

The next time I opened my eyes it was morning and the sun was shining. I could hardly believe the rain had stopped at last. I sat up slowly and was glad to see some of my strength had come back already. Polly was nowhere in sight, but Henry was sitting at the table staring at me.

His hair was even redder than Polly's, and I swear he had freckles on top of freckles on top of freckles.

"I fed your horse some grass," he said. "Your pa must be rich to give you a horse that fine."

I grinned. "My pa isn't rich, and he didn't give me Ranger."

"Then how'd you get him?"

"Let's just say he used to be in the Union Cavalry, but I liberated him."

"You stole him from the Yankees?" Henry's eyes widened in admiration.

It occurred to me I was showing off. Next I'd be telling the boy about Captain Powell's death and my escape from jail. It might be better to keep my mouth shut about some of my deeds. "I found him," I said, "that's all. I guess his owner got killed or something."

"To them Yankees, it's all the same. You could be hung for a horse thief."

"I guess so." I was tired already from sitting up so I rested back on my elbows. "Where's Polly?"

"She's gone down the road to Widow Ransom's place, hoping to talk her out of a few eggs." Henry scowled. "That old lady will make Polly do some chores first. So it may be a while 'fore she comes home."

"How about a drink of water? I'm parched."

Henry jumped up. "Drat. Polly told me to fetch you water and I plumb forgot."

He went out to the well behind the cabin. While he pumped away, I pulled on my clothes, dry now but stained with mud. By the time Henry returned I was dressed and sitting at the table, still feeling a bit trembly and achy. Carefully he filled a cup from the bucket of well water and handed it to me. I was glad to see my hands were steadier.

"There's some porridge left," Henry said, "and some bread. Polly said you can eat if you want."

The porridge wasn't much thicker than water and the bread was hard, but it tasted fine. Soon I was sleeping again.

❖

Polly came home from the widow's with some eggs about the middle of the afternoon. She'd no sooner sat down to rest than we heard the rumble of men and horses coming our way. We stared at each other. "It must be the Yankees," Polly whispered.

As the steady drum of hooves grew louder, Henry grabbed the musket and headed toward the door. Polly stopped him. "Where in tarnation do you think you're going with that gun?"

"I aim to shoot them Bluebellies. Kill as many as I can." While Henry struggled to escape Polly's grip, I grabbed the musket from him. Next thing you'd know, he'd blow somebody's head off. Maybe his own. Maybe mine.

"You ain't going to do nothing of the sort!" Polly yelled. "You'll just get your stupid self kilt, and what good will that do?"

"She's right," I said, keeping the musket out of the boy's reach.

Henry ran to the window and looked out. "They'll be here soon. Can we at least go see them?"

Polly glared at Henry. "If you promise not to do nothing stupid like throwing rocks or hollering insults."

He gave her a sulky look. "Can we loose the dogs on them?"

"You know them hounds won't do nothing. Most likely they'll run off with their tails between their legs, and we won't never see them no more."

Polly turned to me. "You think you got the strength to walk down to the road?"

For a minute I considered staying in the cabin, for there was a chance Major Dennison might be among the soldiers. But I was so caught up in the excitement, I decided he'd be too busy leading his men to notice me.

We made our way down the lane. It was still muddy from the rain, so my shoes suffered somewhat. Neither Polly nor Henry wore anything on their feet. I doubted they had a pair of shoes between them.

I was glad to boost myself onto the fence and sit a spell. Polly sat beside me. Her faded gingham dress was worn so thin I could almost see through it. It was tight, too. The seams strained even though the girl hadn't an extra pound anywhere. I glanced at her feet. They were narrow and freckled. Her second toe was longer than her big toe. First time I'd ever seen that.

"I see their flag!" Henry shouted. "Just coming round the bend up yonder."

What a show those men put on. Though some were old and tired, many were young and fresh and their buttons shone in the sunlight. Their horses pranced and held their heads high. In front of the flag bearers marched a drummer boy and a fifer, both about my age. As they drew near, the boys struck up "The Battle Cry of Freedom," and the soldiers burst into song. With one eye on us, they belted out the chorus.

> *The Union forever,*
> *Hurrah, boys, hurrah!*
> *Down with the traitor,*
> *Up with the star;*
> *While we rally round the flag, boys,*

Rally once again,
Shouting the battle cry of Freedom.

Of course, Henry had to bellow "Dixie." I doubted anyone heard his thin little pipe of voice, but Polly did her best to shush him. She even put her hand over his mouth. Some of the cavalry laughed at the sight of her struggling to control Henry.

One hollered at him. "Hey, boy, you're watching the end of the South pass right in front of your nose."

Of course, Henry slid off the fence and grabbed a rock. "No!" Polly shouted and tackled him. He threw the rock anyway, but it went wide and missed the soldier.

"I seen all I want to see!" Polly gave Henry a shaking hard enough to rattle his teeth and pulled him up the lane toward the cabin. I followed them. I'd seen all I wanted, too.

·18·

WHEN DARKNESS FELL, we ate our supper. Polly scrambled the eggs and cut more hard bread. I wasn't as tired as I had been, so the three of us sat by the fire and talked about our families and the days that used to be. Suddenly, Polly began to sing "Hard Times" in a sweet, quavery voice.

Henry and I joined in the chorus.

'Tis the song, the sigh of the weary;
Hard Times, Hard Times, come again no more.
Many days you have lingered around my cabin door;
Oh! Hard Times, come again no more.

While I sang, I couldn't help recalling the night Mama had sat at our little organ as Rachel, James Marshall, and I sang those very words. We'd all been so happy, never dreaming Hard Times was about to pound on our door and change everything.

When the last chorus was sung, Polly wiped her eyes on her sleeve. "Don't know why I picked that song to sing," she said. "I just opened my mouth and it came spilling out."

"It's a fitting song," I said.

Polly nodded. "Hard Times been knocking on our door for a long while, as far back as I can remember. But now it's worse than ever." She raised her head and stared at me. "You think Hard Times will ever stop his knocking and knocking and knocking?"

It was a tough question. And it required a tough answer. "Even when this war is over," I said slowly, "I believe Hard Times will be knocking on our doors for a long, long time."

Polly lowered her head. "Lord," she murmured, "give us strength."

"Amen," I whispered, for I knew I needed strength as much as she did. And maybe more, because I wasn't used to Hard Times like Polly was. We'd never been rich, but we'd had a sight more comfort and ease than Polly and Henry had ever enjoyed.

"All this sad talk has wore me out." Henry rubbed his eyes and yawned. "I'm so tired I can't hardly see."

"And you, Haswell." Polly turned to me. "You ought to be getting lots of rest. You need to build your strength so's you can go find your brother."

I didn't argue, for I was just as fatigued as Henry. Being up and about had shown me I wasn't quite as fit as I'd thought. I curled up in my blankets and watched Polly and Henry climb the ladder to the loft. "Good night," I called.

Polly paused and smiled down at me. "Sleep well, Haswell."

I nodded, but when I closed my eyes, I saw those Yankees again, marching, marching, marching toward Petersburg. "Please, God," I prayed, "spare Avery's life. Don't let him be killed. Keep him safe from harm. You know Rachel and I can't make it without him."

I knew I had to go on my way soon, but the next day another hard rain commenced. It kept up for three days, flooding fields and roads, making it difficult to go anywhere for several days afterward.

It wasn't just the weather that kept me. My fever lingered, low in the mornings, high in the evenings. Polly fussed over me, but Widow Ransom kept her busy, doing chores in exchange for food.

"That old woman used to have slaves do her work," Henry told me one day while Polly was gone. "But they run off long ago."

"We never had slaves," I said. "Papa thought it was wrong."

"How come he and your brother went off to the fighting, then?" Henry asked.

"To keep the Yankees off our land."

Henry nodded. "That's why Pa went. He didn't care nothing about slavery one way or t'other. He just didn't like Yankees."

We sat quietly for a while, pondering the war. "The Yankees came anyway," Henry said. "And it don't look like they'll be leaving any too soon. Damn them."

He gave me a sly look to see how I felt about swearing. A boy his age, I might have been shocked once but not anymore. When times got this hard, it didn't seem the Lord would mind us cursing every now and then.

"If the Yankees win, does it mean God is on their side?" Henry asked.

"Our preacher said we'd win because God was on *our* side," I said.

"He can't be on both sides." Henry frowned. "Can He?"

"I don't think so."

"But He's God, so's I reckon He could be." Henry sounded puzzled. "He can do anything he pleases."

I thought of Zeus, sitting up there on Mount Olympus watching the Greeks and the Trojans killing each other on the bloody plains of Ilium. He had his favorites. Achilles, for instance. But he let him die. And Hector—who, as Papa said, was a far better man than Achilles.

"Sometimes I think we can't know God's mind any more than Job could. Not you and me. Not preachers, either." I studied Henry's freckled face. "God is God, and only He knows the whys and wherefores of things here on earth."

"That's why I don't plan to go to church no more," Henry said. "Though Polly will probably drag me there as long as she's able. But one day I'll be too big for her to handle, and I'll go off on my own."

He looked at me hard. "How about you, Haswell? You plan to listen to preachers anymore?"

"I don't know about church and preachers and all that," I said slowly. "But I aim to keep on praying."

"Huh," Henry said. "I prayed hard for Mama, and look what happened. She died anyway. The preacher said it was God's will. That's when I quit listening to preachers."

Henry's talk was starting to worry me. I'd read my Bible all my life, and I'd said my prayers and I'd gone to church every Sunday till our preacher went off to join the army. I didn't understand the Lord, but I wasn't about to give up on Him.

"You're hardly more than a child, Henry. It's not right for you to be so—"

"I ain't no child," Henry said.

"Then what are you? I don't see a beard or any other sign of manhood."

To my surprise, Henry's eyes brimmed with tears. "I don't rightly know what I am," he said. "I ain't a child, I ain't a man. I'm just me, and I seen what I seen and I know what I know."

He jumped up from the table and went to the window, looking for his sister, I guessed. Also hiding his tears. "Here comes Polly," he said, "running like the devil hisself was chasing her."

Polly burst into the cabin. Her hair was working its way out of her braids, one curly red strand after another, and her cheeks were flushed pink. She looked like she'd run all the way from the widow's house.

"Richmond's surrendered!" she cried. "And Petersburg, too. There's Yankees everywhere."

Speechless, I stared at Polly. Richmond? It couldn't be. Not the capital of the Confederacy. And if Petersburg had fallen, how was I to find Avery? What if he'd been wounded in the fighting? Or killed?

While I stood there as mute as a fool, Henry ran to Polly's side and grabbed her shoulders as if he meant to shake her. "Where in tarnation did you hear that? It's a lie, a damnable, outrageous lie!"

Polly pulled away from him. "It's true, Henry, I swear to God. A Confederate officer came by the widow's house and told us."

"He's a liar," Henry said.

"No, he was a messenger, sending news for us to be ready for battle. He says it's bound to come this way." Polly began to cry then. "What shall we do?"

Polly's news shouldn't have shocked me. Any fool could tell the war wasn't going well for us. It was like the night Grandpa Colby died. He'd been sick so long everybody knew he'd die. But when he actually stopped breathing, we were all as shocked as if he'd been killed by lightning. That was how I felt now. Dumbstruck and heartsick and scared.

"Why does he think the fighting will come this away?" Henry asked.

"He didn't say." Polly wrung her long, thin hands together. "But if it does come, this cabin ain't safe. We can't stay here."

"We'll go to Widow Ransom's house," Henry said. "She likes you, Polly. She'll take us in. She's been wanting to ever since Pa left."

"Yes, but I was hoping to stay on our own, not be obligated to anyone." Polly held up her chin. It shook in spite of her effort to look brave. "But I can't think of nothing else to do."

I got to my feet, cursing the weakness that lingered in my legs. "Polly, I can't stay here. I have to find Avery. What if he gets killed in the fighting?"

"No, Haswell!" she cried. "Don't go. Not with the soldiers heading this way." She gave me a shake, as if I were Henry's age. "Look at you, still ailing. Why, your fever will come right back. And then where will you be?"

I tried to pull loose, but Polly was a sight stronger than she looked.

"Please stay here," Polly begged. "Please, Haswell."

I felt both perplexed and confused, standing so close to Polly and feeling her hands holding fast to my arms. Her eyes were level with mine, greeny gray and sadder than ever. Her red hair hung in wispy curls around her face. I found myself stammering when I told her, all right, I'd stay, but just a little longer.

Polly sighed and released me. Her face was almost as red as her hair. "I reckon I better cook supper. It's getting dark."

She turned away and took three eggs and a loaf of bread from the basket she'd brought from the widow's house.

Henry sighed. "I'm powerful weary of scrambled eggs, Polly. Can you fry them this time?"

Polly glanced at me. "If it's all right with Haswell."

"It's fine," I said. "I'll eat anything you care to cook and be grateful for it."

Polly blushed again.

"I'm going to see to Ranger," I said.

Outside the evening was cool and the stars hung bright and sharp in the sky. A long way off, an owl hooted, too far away to be calling my name. The peepers kept up their endless chirping down in the marshy places. I looked up at the moon and wished the night were as ordinary as it seemed.

But somewhere under that very same moon soldiers huddled by fires, waiting for morning, Avery among them. Maybe he was looking at the moon, too, thinking of Mama and Rachel and me gathered round the table, eating supper. Poor Avery. There was so much he didn't know.

And I was the one who would have to tell him.

·19·

THE NEXT MORNING we were sitting at the table eating our grits when, suddenly, Henry raised his head. "Do you hear thunder?"

I laid down my spoon and listened. "It's gunfire and cannons," I said.

Polly leapt up, her face so white her freckles popped out. "Is it heading this way?"

Henry and I ran outside. Far across the rolling hills and fields, we saw smoke pluming like gray clouds against the blue sky. The gunfire was getting louder.

"They're in the woods over on the other side of Cooper's farm," Henry said. "I wager they'll be coming right across his fields toward us."

We hurried back to the cabin. Polly was waiting on the porch, her apron scrunched in her hands. "Are they coming?" she called.

"I believe so!" I shouted.

I'd no sooner spoken than a dozen or so Confederate soldiers came dashing out of the woods, putting their feet to it as hard as they could. They weren't more than a half mile away and heading straight toward the cabin. Union soldiers burst out of the woods in pursuit, dozens of them—maybe hundreds—coming from everywhere.

"Go to the widow's house! Run!" I yelled at Polly. "I'll get Ranger."

"Set the hounds loose, Henry!" Polly shouted.

While Henry opened the pen's gate, I ran into the cabin and grabbed my revolver. Then, fumble-fingered with fear, I saddled Ranger. I swear I could almost see Death coming, a tall, gaunt figure dressed in black rags. His head blotted out the sun. His scythe flashed like lightning, cutting down soldiers like wheat at harvest time.

I leapt onto Ranger's back. The hounds scattered around me, streaking toward the woods as fast as they could go, their bellies grazing the grass. It was clear they wanted none of the war.

By the time I was clear of the stableyard, the field behind me had become a battle scene. Men were shooting, screaming, falling. The Confederates couldn't hold. Some tried. They were outnumbered, but they kept on shooting. Others dropped their guns and ran.

With gunfire ringing out, I galloped after Henry and Polly. They were running uphill toward the widow's fine old stone house. Polly was carrying the musket.

I slowed down beside them. "You go on to the house," I said. "I'm going to hole up in the barn with Ranger."

Polly and Henry didn't answer, but they swerved away from the house and followed me. Their contrariness riled me somewhat, for I was thinking of their safety, but the barn was solid stone, too, almost as big as the house and just as solid. It was cool and dark inside, smelling of hay and horses, though those things were long gone.

Ranger resisted me. He pawed the ground, he whinnied, he reared up as if he meant to fight his way out of the barn. Finally, I got him into a stall and bolted the door.

He kicked and carried on, acting even more ugly than he had for Captain Dennison in Winchester.

Henry gazed at the horse in awe. "He wants to go to war," he said. "That's what they trained him for."

"He's not going anywhere," I said. "And neither are you," I added, for it occurred to me Henry would like nothing more than to ride Ranger into battle.

Polly grabbed Henry's arm and held it tight. "They're getting closer, Haswell. What will we do if they come in here?"

"Shoot them if they're Yankees," Henry said. "Ain't that right, Haswell?"

"Only if we have to." The thought of shooting a man made my stomach quiver.

"Oh, Lord, preserve us!" Polly cried as the loudest noise I'd ever heard boomed over our heads. A shell had struck the barn high up and made a hole in the wall big enough to see the sky.

Two more shells broke holes in the wall. Chunks of stone and rubble came rattling down all around us, striking our shoulders and backs and heads. Dust rose and we choked and coughed. Ranger stamped his feet and whinnied.

The sounds of the battle grew louder. Soon I could make out shouts, screams, horses whinnying.

Henry scrambled up the ladder to the loft. "We can watch through the hole the shell made."

I followed him, but Polly stayed below. She had a good grip on the musket to prove she was ready to do whatever she had to.

Outside, Confederate soldiers came running across the field, mostly unarmed, stumbling, shoving one another aside. I watched them go by, my heart sinking fast at the sight of our army in full retreat.

Henry gripped my arm hard. "They're running," he whispered. "They're running, Haswell. Why ain't they shooting those sons of guns?"

"Look at them." I pointed to ranks of Union soldiers charging out of the woods in all directions. "How can we fight that many Yankees?"

Henry pressed his head against the barn's wall. His shoulders shook and I knew he was crying, but I didn't shame him by saying so. Besides, I was so worried Avery was among those fleeing soldiers I couldn't think about anything else. Lord, Lord, I prayed, don't let them kill Avery. Please, Lord, keep him safe, spread your shield over him.

Another wave of Confederates came into sight, still firing. They'd turn and shoot, run, shoot again, run some more. Officers on horseback moved in and out among the men, urging them to stand and fight.

It occurred to me the barn wasn't as safe as I'd thought. What if the fleeing soldiers ran inside to escape the Yankees? Why, Polly and Henry and I would die with them.

The Confederates dashed into the widow's yard. Near the barn, they formed a ragged line and returned the Yankees' fire. The air filled with smoke and dust. I couldn't see who was who. Rifles blazed, men screamed and fell. A minié ball whistled over my head and struck the wall behind me.

On the grass below my vantage point, a man took a shot in the head. He tumbled off his horse, spraying blood as he fell. The horse screamed and went down, shot, too. In his stall, Ranger answered the dying horse with a loud whinny.

It was hard to believe any soldier, North or South, would live to see the sun set. Yet they kept on shooting and yelling as if they aimed to kill everyone but themselves. Bullets whined past the barn. Some hit the stone walls, some hit trees, but none hit Henry or me. All I could think was, "Make it stop, dear Jesus in heaven, make it stop."

But it didn't stop, and it wouldn't stop till it was done.

Suddenly, I heard Polly call my name. I crawled to the edge of the loft and peered down at her. "A soldier," she said. "He's wounded."

I looked where she pointed.

A soldier had staggered into the barn. He was covered with dirt and blood. I couldn't tell if he was a Yankee or a Confederate. But he was dying, I was sure of it.

He stood by the door, unarmed and bleeding badly. "Please?" he whispered to Polly and held out one arm to her. "Please?"

Before any of us could speak or move, the soldier collapsed and fell to the floor.

Henry and I scrambled down the ladder.

"Is he dead?" Henry asked me.

"I don't know."

Polly knelt by the soldier. His eyelids fluttered and he looked up at her. "Don't let me die, not now, not after all I been through."

She took his hand and held tight. "You're safe here," she whispered.

The soldier seized Polly and pressed his face to her breast. "Please, dear Lord," he prayed, "let me see my mother's face just once more. My home. My . . ."

He began to shiver and then to shake, but his grip on Polly never loosened. Blood ran from his mouth. He struggled hard to breathe, held Polly so tight I thought her dress would rip.

"Mother," he groaned. "Mother."

I heard the death rattle begin. He shook harder. His heels drummed against the floor. His body stiffened. Still holding Polly, he died.

"Oh, Haswell." Polly looked up at me, tears streaming down her face. "The poor young man. Oh, the poor, poor, young man." She held him, her own dress soaked through with his blood, and cried as if she'd never stop.

The blood on her dress and her tears brought Mama to mind. Surely Polly wouldn't go crazy, too. She hadn't killed the soldier. She'd comforted him at his dying, which was a good thing to do.

"What are you crying for?" Henry asked. "He's a Yankee, Polly. See his blue coat?"

"It don't matter what he is," Polly said, holding the soldier tight, "except he's too young to die and his mama don't even know he's gone."

"Polly." I touched her shoulder. "Put him down. You can't help him now."

Polly cradled the soldier. "His spirit might be here, watching, seeking comfort."

"Polly!" Henry tugged at his sister. "Let him go now, let him go!"

"Please, Polly," I said. "You can't do anything for him."

At last Polly untangled herself from the soldier's embrace and laid him gently on the barn floor. We all stared at the terrible gaping wound in his chest.

"For a Yankee, he was brave enough," Henry said. "He took that bullet from the front."

I reckoned that was the biggest compliment a dead Yankee could expect to receive from Henry.

"Poor young man." Polly gazed at him a moment. "We don't even know his Christian name. I wish—"

A shell exploded and drowned out the rest of Polly's words. The three of us flinched. As stones rained from the barn wall, Polly dropped down beside the dead soldier and covered her ears.

"Get under that wagon!" I shouted. Polly and Henry followed me, and we dove into the darkness and cobwebs and huddled there together. In his stall Ranger reared and pawed at the air with his hooves.

I didn't know about Polly and Henry, but the same thoughts ran through my head, one after another, spinning round and round as if they were tied together. First I'd pray to God to spare our lives; then I'd pray for Avery; then I'd think about dying and pray to God to forgive me all my sins so I could cross the river and join Mama and Papa in the shade of the trees. Oh, but I didn't want to die, so I'd begin my prayers all over again.

Just when I thought I couldn't bear it any longer, the battle noise began to fade away. Slowly, slowly, like the sun going down and the sky growing dark and the stars coming out, one by one.

When we were sure the battle was really over, we crawled out from under the wagon. To my relief Ranger had calmed down. He seemed almost like his normal self but a bit more restless than usual. I decided to leave him where he was for now. No sense riling him up again.

Slowly we pushed the barn door open and peered out. Partly hidden by smoke, dead soldiers and horses sprawled on the widow's lawn. Wounded men groaned and cried out. Some staggered around, calling names, searching for friends.

It was a hideous sight, worse than anything I'd ever imagined. We turned our eyes away, even Henry.

"Please, miss," a soldier called to Polly. "Can you bring me water?" He leaned on one elbow, too weak to sit up. His head was bleeding and his uniform was torn and bloody.

Others began calling out, pleading for water, for help. Those hurt too bad to speak just moaned and groaned. They lay among the silent dead, who needed nothing now but a decent burial.

Polly gazed at the soldiers, her face filled with sorrow and pity. "Go to the widow's well," she told Henry and me. "Fill the bucket."

While Polly moved among the men, inquiring about their injuries, Henry and I went to the well and began hoisting the bucket. Soon we were ladling water to the wounded, doing our best to ease their suffering. For once Henry had nothing to say about Yankees.

As we were drawing a third bucket from the well, two Union officers rode toward us. Behind them lumbered a wagon fixed up as a field hospital. Without giving us a glance, they galloped past and dismounted near the house.

"Is this your home, miss?" one asked Polly.

"No, sir, it belongs to the Widow Ransom."

"Is she here?"

"I reckon so." Polly paused and looked hard at the officer. "That is, if you ain't killed her with all that shelling."

Polly had something there. The widow's house had been hit almost as bad as the barn. There was a big hole in the second story. You could see the bedroom itself—or what was left of it. The bed, the chest of drawers, the flowered wallpaper. The porch columns were scarred with bullets. Windows were broken. One chimney leaned crazily to the side, ready to collapse.

The captain strode up to the widow's back door and banged loudly. "Open up," he called. "This is Major Brannon of the New York Thirty-Third. We're requisitioning your house for a hospital."

The door slowly opened, and an old lady peered out. She scanned the yard, taking in the dreadful scene. When her eyes lit on Polly, Henry, and me, she cried out, "Is that you Polly O'Brien? Land sakes, I'm glad to see you, child! I reckoned you and Henry was kilt for sure."

The Widow Ransom looked at me, then back to Polly. "Who's that raggedy boy? And where did he come from?"

"Why, this here's Haswell Magruder from up Winchester way," Polly said. "He's looking for his brother."

Major Brannon stepped closer to Widow Ransom. "Ma'am, we need your house to treat these men. Will you kindly allow us to bring them inside?"

I must say he asked in a polite way. He even took off his hat and held it to his breast, as a gentleman should.

"Yankees in my house?" Widow Ransom frowned and drew herself up as tall as a tiny woman can. "What would my poor deceased husband say?"

"I don't think it matters what a dead man would say," snapped Major Brannon. I guessed his manners were no more than show after all.

The two of them looked each other in the eye, the widow peering up, the major peering down. On the grass the wounded men groaned and cried and prayed.

Polly ran up to the door and took the widow's hand. "Mrs. Ransom, I think you should do what he says. Them soldiers are Confederates as well as Yankees. They need help bad."

The widow turned to Major Brannon. "You aim to treat our boys as well as yours?"

He nodded. "Yes, ma'am."

The old woman stepped aside. "You may do as you wish, sir. But please be careful of my home. Treat it as you would your own house."

The men from the hospital wagon had already begun loading men on stretchers. While we stood watching, they carried them inside. No matter how careful the stretcher bearers were, the men cried out at every jolt and bump.

"Polly." The widow touched Polly's arm. "Will you stay and help? These boys will need bandages. Perhaps you and Henry could busy yourselves tearing bed linens into strips. And you, Haswell, you could fetch water from the well."

I hesitated. How was I to say no? Yet how could I stay? The Lord only knew where Avery might be. In the barn, I heard Ranger whinny.

"I'd like to help, ma'am," I said as politely as I could, "but I need to be on my way. I have to find my brother."

Polly's face reddened, but she didn't say a word, didn't even look at me. She stood there picking at her fingernails like she didn't know what else to do with herself.

I went to the barn and led Ranger out. He was still tense and edgy, so I mounted quickly and rode back to Polly. She was standing on the widow's porch, and her face was level with mine. She was so close I could see tears shining on her eyelashes.

"Are you coming back this way, Haswell?" She didn't look at me, just stood there with her head down, twirling a strand of red hair round and round her finger till the skin turned white from the pressure.

"No," I told her. "My home's to the west and north from here. But I, I—I'll see you again sometime, Polly. Honest, I will."

She looked at me, her lips parted as if she wanted to speak but couldn't. I leaned over and kissed her on the mouth. I hadn't planned to. I'd never kissed a girl in my whole entire life, hadn't even thought about it. But just then it seemed the most natural thing in the world to do.

Polly touched her lips. "Oh," she said. "Oh."

"Polly," the widow called from the house. "Get in here. Henry's doing his best to tear up the linens, but he needs help!"

I took a chance and kissed Polly again. This time she kissed me back. "You're the prettiest girl in the whole world," I told her. "And I thank you kindly for all you've done to help me."

She blushed so red her freckles disappeared. "You must be needing spectacles," she whispered. "Else you ain't seen many girls."

"Boy, get that horse out of here," a soldier yelled at me. "Can't you see you're in our way?"

"Yes, sir." I turned Ranger reluctantly. I backed away slowly, keeping my eyes on Polly.

"Be careful," Polly called. "Don't get yourself shot or nothing."

"You be careful, too, Polly." I nudged Ranger's sides with my heels, and he broke into a trot, obviously more eager to leave than I was.

Polly ran partway down the lane behind me, waving hard. "Don't forget me!"

Henry chased after her, shouting, "Wait up, Haswell, wait up! Don't you want me to help you find Avery?"

I saw Polly grab Henry and hold him tight. "You ain't going nowhere, you stubborn little fool!"

I wished I could take them both. But Ranger couldn't carry the three of us, at least not very far or very fast.

So I rode on, giving Ranger his head. Soon a tree blocked my view of Polly and Henry. Then they were gone, and the road lay ahead of me.

The wind blew, stirring the trees. Somewhere a pair of jays squabbled. A stream along the side of the road gurgled and murmured as it went on its way. But there wasn't a person or a house in sight. Just unplowed fields stretching away under a cloudy sky.

Loneliness pressed down on me, emptying me of everything but fear. What if Avery were dead? What would happen to the farm? To my sister and me?

I sent a silent prayer up to the Lord, once more asking His help, and rode on toward the next town.

·20·

In a few minutes it became clear I was following the same route as the retreat. The Confederates must have come across the fields and run into more Yankees on the road. Union and Confederate soldiers sprawled where they'd fallen among dead horses, smashed carts and wagons, and abandoned supplies. Blood soaked into the ground and pooled in puddles. Fires smoldered here and there on the grassy banks. The air stank so of death and gunsmoke I could hardly breathe for choking.

Hordes of flies buzzed around the bodies, bloating themselves as they fed. Crows hopped about, pecking and pulling at the corpses, fighting among themselves, too bold to be afraid of me. Overhead, buzzards circled, waiting their turn.

At first I searched the dead soldiers' faces, fearing I'd find Avery among them. The agony I saw soon made me stop looking. I prayed to the Lord again. "Please let me find Avery alive, not among the dead."

With that I nudged Ranger and we increased our speed until we'd left most of the dead behind.

At twilight I rounded a curve in the road and came in sight of the Confederate prisoners. There must have been thousands of them, huddled together in a field outside a town. Appomattox, I learned later.

I sat there on Ranger, in plain sight, and watched the men. They didn't appear to notice me. Some lay on the ground, their eyes closed, haggard and weary, no fight left. Others sat and talked in low voices or walked about aimlessly. Most looked like men waking from a dream to find themselves in a place they'd never seen. "Where am I?" they seemed to ask. "And how did I get here?"

Gradually the sky faded into night. I led Ranger into the woods across the road and dismounted. Every bone in my body ached. I was weary and hungry and sad. I rolled up in my blanket and lay down in the grass, wishing Polly and Henry were with me. I hoped they were safe at the widow's house, that she'd keep them and care for them until their father came home from the war. If he ever did.

I hadn't given poor Rachel much thought lately, but lying alone in that empty field, I saw her as I'd seen her last, sleeping with her hair spread out, the very picture of Mama. I had no idea how she'd managed living with Grandma Colby all this time. If I knew Rachel, she was giving the old lady fits. But I reckoned she was unhappy and lonesome and pretty angry at me for leaving her there. Yes, sir, when I rode into Winchester, I was going to get quite a reception from both Rachel and Grandma Colby.

It was full dark now, not the moon or a star to be seen, but in the field across road the watch fires burned.

The Yankees began singing the national anthem. Very faintly at first but growing louder as more voices joined in, the Confederates came back with "Dixie." The Yankees sang the "The Battle Hymn of the Republic," and the Confederates countered with "The Bonnie Blue Flag." I fell asleep wishing wars could be fought with songs instead of bullets.

Day dawned gray and cool. The wind carried the smell of cooking fires, and my nose filled with the mouth-watering smell of bacon and coffee. In the field the prisoners had formed long raggedy lines. They waited patiently, heads down, as if eating was something they had to do but didn't much care about. My stomach growled. I had nothing but a half a loaf of bread and a wrinkled apple. I gave Ranger the last of his oats and the apple as well. I made do with the bread.

When I'd eaten the last crumb, I filled my canteen at a creek and mounted Ranger. What I needed was news. For all I knew the war was over and done with and all those prisoners would soon be released. If Avery was amongst them, I wanted to find him before he wandered off somewhere.

In town, people thronged the streets, mobbing the courthouse steps, shouting and yelling. Church bells tolled. Children cried and covered their ears against the uproar.

"You heard the news, boy?" A plump woman grabbed Ranger's saddle and stared up at me. Tears ran down her cheeks. "General Robert E. Lee has surrendered to Grant. He's disbanded the Army of Northern Virginia."

I sat on Ranger's back and stared at the woman. Crowds thronged around us, jostling the horse. "You mean the war's over?"

"In Virginia it is," she said. "Lee surrendered. Nobody else has that I know of. Mosby's still up in the mountains somewheres."

A tall, hawk-eyed man pushed the woman aside. "Mexico," he hollered. "Lee's a-going to Mexico. The army will come back, ten thousand strong, and whup them Yankees."

"Mexico." A fat man in a ragged frock spat in the dust. "Nah, them boys is heading for the hills. They'll join up with Mosby and keep fighting."

"You two are crazy as loons," a dignified man spoke up. "Grant's pardoned Lee. He ain't hanging anybody. Why, he's even allowing soldiers to keep their guns and horses. You think any of them men got the spirit to keep fighting?" He pointed to the road behind me.

I turned and saw the prisoners shuffling toward us. They looked used up, spent, like walking dead men.

The crowd parted to let them through, calling out words of comfort, offering water, reaching out to shake their hands. "Poor boys," a woman whispered to her friend. The other woman wiped her tears away with her apron. "At least they're alive, they're going home," she said.

As the prisoners passed me, I slid off Ranger's back and grabbed one by the arm. "Do you know Avery Magruder? Have you seen him?"

He shook his head and pulled away. But I kept at it, stopping as many of them as I could and asking about Avery. Some didn't say anything. They mumbled and walked on past as if I weren't there at all. A few expressed interest in my horse. One or two offered to buy him. No one threatened to kill me or tried to take Ranger by force. I don't believe they had the energy. Like me, they just wanted to go home.

When I'd just about given up hope of finding my brother, a red-headed man stopped. He was as battle-worn as the others, but his eyes were kind. "Avery Magruder," he said. "Are you kin to him?"

"I'm his brother, Haswell." My heart beat so fast I almost choked on my words. "Avery was at Petersburg during the siege."

The soldier nodded his head. "Yes," he said. "Yes. I fought along side of him at Farmville."

"Where is he now?" I grabbed hold of the man so tight he tottered and almost fell.

"Why, I can't say, Haswell. We were separated during the retreat, and I haven't seen him since. If Avery was wounded, he'd be in the hospital tents." The man pointed back the way he'd come. "In the Yankee camp. They've got their hands full, those doctors. Must be thousands of wounded, both Yankee and Confederate."

I thanked him kindly and shook the hand he held out.

"Avery was a good soldier," he said. "A good man. I hope you find him." Giving my hand a last squeeze, he turned and went on his way.

I watched him for a moment. He'd called Avery a good man. Not a boy. A man. A little shiver ran over my skin. Just a year ago Avery had been a boy like me. How had he become a man so fast?

The hospital camp was just over the hill. It was almost dark, so the tents were lit with lanterns. The canvas sides glowed orange like harvest moons. Here and there camp-fires flickered.

I led Ranger into the woods and tied him to a tree, well out of sight of the road. "Stay right here, fellow. Don't let anybody steal you away." I pressed my face against his. "I'll be back soon."

I left him munching weeds and ventured down into the camp. Men were cooking supper, but the smell of food didn't cover the stench of death. The evening air was full of it. Outside one tent was a hideous sight—amputated arms and legs piled in heaps higher than my head. I turned my face away, sickened by the sight.

From one of the tents, I heard a man scream, "Don't cut it off! Oh, God, let me keep my leg. Don't let them take it."

At the same time, two soldiers carried a dead man past me and laid him in a row of corpses waiting for burial, lines and lines of them. I hurried past the bodies, fearful of seeing Avery amongst them.

Near a hospital tent, a doctor stood in the shadows, smoking a cigar and studying the stars. His apron was dark with blood, and so were the sleeves of his shirt. In truth he looked more like a butcher than a surgeon.

I touched his arm. "Pardon me, sir," I whispered, "I've come in search of my brother. Someone told me he might be here among the wounded."

The doctor glared down at me as if I'd interrupted an important thought. "Southerner?"

"Yes, sir. His name's Avery Magruder, sir. He's sixteen years old. Tall. Blond hair. Have you seen him?"

"Look here," he said. "We've got hundreds of casualties, ours and yours both. Do you actually think I know their names?"

I grabbed his arm to keep him from walking away. "How am I to find him? Or even know if he's here?"

The doctor flung me off impatiently. "You could start by going from tent to tent. If you don't see him among the wounded, look for him among the dead. Many a man lost his life today. More will join them tomorrow."

So saying, the doctor extinguished his cigar and disappeared into a tent.

Since I could think of nothing else to do, I followed his advice and followed him. In the dim light the wounded lay on pallets of straw, crowded as close to one another as kernels on a corncob. The air stank of human filth and blood and rotting wounds. The men tossed and turned and begged for water. They cursed their pain, cursed the war, cursed their officers. Some prayed to Jesus. Others called for their mothers, their wives, their sweethearts. I truly felt I was in hell, listening to the cries of the damned.

Though it put me close to retching, I walked among the men, studying their faces. Their bandages were bloodstained, their bodies little more than skeletons. Fearing I might not recognize Avery, I forced myself to walk slower, to stare at the men even more intently.

Most took no notice of me. I was simply another stranger passing among them. Once in a while, a man would ask me what the devil I was looking at, and I'd tell him I was searching for Avery Magruder. He'd shake his head and wish me luck. Or curse me.

There were eight tents in all. It was in the seventh that I found Avery.

·21·

At first I wasn't certain the soldier was actually my brother or a pale and sickly copy of the Avery I remembered. His head was wrapped in a bloody bandage, he'd grown a shaggy beard, and his skin was gray with dirt. But worst of all was the expression on his face. Dull. Blank. Vacant. Like a deserted building with dark windows, emptied out and hollow.

It would have broken Mama's heart to see him, her firstborn son, the joy of her heart, looking so different from the boy she'd raised.

I leaned closer, staring hard at Avery, trying to see his chest rise and fall. From his appearance, it was hard to tell if he were alive or dead.

I reached out fearfully and touched his shoulder. "Avery," I whispered, "it's me, Haswell. I've come to fetch you home."

To my relief he opened his eyes and stared at my face as if he were struggling to recollect me. Maybe he'd seen me before, maybe he hadn't. He didn't seem altogether certain of anything.

"I'm your brother, Avery," I tried again. "Haswell Magruder."

He nodded, but his eyes were still vacant. "Haswell," he repeated. "Haswell Magruder, my brother."

I took hold of his hands and squeezed hard. "Please, Avery, try and remember. I've come such a long way to find you."

Avery's eyes settled on my face. He held my hands so tight, I thought my bones would splinter like matchsticks. "It *is* you," he said hoarsely. "It truly is. Lord, I thought I was dreaming."

He reached up and pulled me to him. My head rested on his chest. I could smell days of sweat mixed with the odor of gunpowder and stale blood. It seemed he'd never let me go.

Not that I cared. I didn't want to let him go, either. I'd been searching for him so long and I was tired, so tired. Weary to my very soul.

At last Avery let me go but he held on to my hands. I straightened up so I could see his face.

"What are you doing here, Haswell?" he asked. "Mama would never allow you to come so far. Surely you haven't run away to join the army. The war's just about over."

I looked down at our clasped hands. Strange to say, mine were almost as big as his now. When had that happened? I guessed I'd been too busy to notice I'd grown.

"What is it, Haswell?" Avery's voice shook with fear. "For God's sake, what's happened? Tell me."

Mute, I shook my head. As long as Avery didn't know otherwise, Mama was still alive, at least in his mind. It was like killing her all over again to say she was dead.

"I came to get you because, because . . . " I turned my head away. "Oh, Avery, don't make me say it."

"She's dead," he whispered. "Mama's dead."

I wiped my eyes on my sleeve. "She died of fever. In February." I didn't want to tell him about the Yankees and what they'd done. Or what she'd done to the captain. Not yet.

Avery hid his face in his hands. Without looking at me, he said, "Rachel, is she . . . is she gone, too?"

"Oh, no, Rachel's as right as rain," I said, relieved to have some good news. "I left her at Uncle Cornelius's house, along with Grandma Colby and the aunts. I reckon she's fuming mad at me for leaving her there."

He lowered his hands and stared at me. "Who's tending the farm?"

"There's no farm to tend," I admitted. "The Yankees burned everything, even the house. They took all the livestock, too. We've got nothing left, Avery. I don't know what we're going to do." My voice broke, and I blinked hard to keep from crying. Hard as it was, I had to be a man now like Avery.

Avery surprised me with a string of curse words. Against the war, against himself, against the whole world and all the fools in it. He'd never been the sort of boy who swore. Papa would never have tolerated such language. Nor Mama, either.

"All that's kept me alive is the thought of seeing Mama again," Avery went on. "I meant to tell her she was right. I should have stayed home. If I had, she'd be alive right now."

I winced for he seemed to be saying if he'd been home, things would have been different. And who knows? He could be right. "But you weren't there," I said. "And neither was Papa. It was just Rachel and me. We did our best, but Mama was sick and we couldn't make her better."

"I'm certain you did all you could, Haswell," he said. "I'm not blaming you. I only meant that . . . " He touched the bandage swathing his head and frowned. "A damnable Yankee cavalryman almost split my skull open with his saber. Sometimes my head aches so fierce I can't think straight." His voice was low and I had to lean close to his mouth to hear him.

Avery took my hand in his and lay back. "Let me sleep a while, Haswell. Let me rest." He closed his eyes and dropped into sleep as fast as a stone disappears when it's dropped into a pond. For the first time tonight he looked almost like himself. But maybe it was just because his eyes were shut and I couldn't see the darkness in them.

I sat beside my brother, watching and worrying, holding his hand tight. All around me, soldiers sighed and moaned. A few rows away a man kept crying out, "Oh, God, take me, let me die. I can't bear it no more." Others wept. One sang hymns in a broken voice, forgetting the words, straying from the tune, then starting all over only to falter in the same places again and again.

Around dawn two orderlies in bloody aprons came in and took stock of things. They gave water to those who wanted it and took away the bodies of those who'd died in the night.

When they came to Avery's cot, he stirred and opened his eyes. "Water," he whispered.

I watched him sip a few mouthfuls from a tin ladle and then lie back. Before he closed his eyes, he saw me and blinked.

"Haswell," he murmured. "You're still here." He made an effort to smile, but it was more of a grimace than anything else. "You've grown some."

I nodded. "Are you well enough to travel?"

Avery made an effort to sit up. "You mean go home?"

"What's left of it."

Judging by the look on his face, I reckoned he'd forgotten what I'd told him last night. He bent over and clutched the sides of his head, but he didn't say a thing. Just rocked back and forth like a man in the grip of a misery too bad for words.

I touched his shoulder, and he grabbed my hand and squeezed hard. He still said nothing. I didn't say anything, either, for I was in the grip of the same misery.

After a while Avery released my hand and shoved the blankets aside. He fumbled for a faded jacket and a pair of ragged trousers. The effort of dressing seemed to exhaust him. He sat on the edge of the cot, breathing hard, his face dripping with perspiration.

"Are you sure you can travel?" I asked. "You look poorly, Avery."

"I am poorly, Haswell, and have been for a long while, even before I was struck on the head."

My heart slowed in dread. "Should we stay here till you feel stronger?"

Avery shook his head. With great effort, he rose to his feet and stood there, as wobbly as a baby learning to walk. He put out a skinny hand and leaned on my shoulder. "I want to go home," he whispered and took a small faltering step. "Or die trying."

"Your boots," I said. "Where are they?"

Avery gave me a puzzled look. "Boots? I haven't had boots for months. I don't know what happened to them. They wore out, I reckon."

Barefoot and gaunt, he shuffled beside me, leaning hard on my shoulder with his right hand, more like an old man than my big brother. I wished I'd brought Ranger into camp so Avery wouldn't have to walk so far. But most likely someone would have stolen him. And then we would've had to walk all the way to Winchester.

Outside the tent a Yankee sentry stepped into our path. "Where are you going?" His voice was tired, his face lined.

From the look of him, he didn't care what Avery answered.

"Home to my farm." Avery's voice was as weary as the sentry's.

The two men looked each other over, their faces expressionless. "Go on, then," the sentry said, jerking his thumb toward the road. "The war's over, at least in Virginia."

We did as the sentry said, Avery and I. He walked slowly, still leaning on me, breathing hard. I could feel him trembling with the effort. The morning was gray and cold—typical April weather. Mist rose from the fields, and the air smelled of damp earth. When we drew near the place I'd hidden Ranger, I told Avery to sit on the ground and rest a minute. He sank down slowly and looked up at me. His eyes seemed unnaturally blue in his dirty face. "Don't be gone too long," he murmured.

I made my way into the woods, brushing aside branches and the cobwebs strung between them. All the time my heart was heavy with fear Ranger would be gone. Stolen. Run away. Lost.

But for once my fears were wasted. Ranger stood where I'd left him, quietly cropping weeds. He raised his head when he heard me and pawed the ground. I thanked the Lord for keeping Ranger safe and hugged the horse tight.

A few minutes later I called to Avery, who seemed to be asleep in the grass. He sat up with effort and stared at me. "Where the devil did you get that horse, Haswell?"

"It's a long story," I said. "But he's a fine animal, isn't he? I call him Ranger, after Mosby's men."

With a boost from me, Avery tried to climb on Ranger's back. It was a real struggle for both of us. Avery was weak but taller than I was, and he seemed to have lost his coordination. His legs flopped, he slid this way and that, land-ing on the grass more than once. Ranger bore it well. Maybe he thought it was a new game.

When Avery was finally in place, too exhausted to say a word, I led the horse down the road at a slow pace. I didn't want Avery to fall off. We'd used up a lot of our strength getting him in the saddle.

Sometime in the afternoon, we saw two soldiers ahead, Confederates making their way home like us. When they stopped to rest, we caught up with them. One was named Sykes, a stretched-out, reedy fellow with a deathly pale face. The other's name was Phillips. He was as short and stout as his friend was tall and thin. They made an odd pair, limping along together.

Phillips eyed Ranger. "That's a mighty fine horse," he said.

"Yes, indeed he is," Sykes agreed. "You're fortunate to have him."

It always made me uneasy when people overly admired my horse. I drew closer to him and rested my hand lightly on his neck.

"Don't worry, son," Sykes said. "We don't aim to steal him. We're just two old soldiers hoping to get home afore we die."

"Keep us company for a while," Phillips suggested.

Soon the pair was telling Avery about their battles. "We fought at Cold Harbor," Sykes said.

Avery shuddered. "That's one I'm glad to have missed."

"Wish we'd missed it, too," said Phillips.

"Before that, we was at the Wilderness and Spotsylvania," Sykes told us. "Thought we'd seen bad fighting there, but Cold Harbor—" He broke off and coughed, a loose nasty sound that called Otis Hicks to mind.

"They just kept on coming," Phillips went on, "those

—— *185* ——

crazy Feds, and we just kept shooting them. Waves and waves of them. The North must have a powerful lot of men to throw them away like that."

"Petersburg wasn't any picnic," Avery put in. "Nor was what came after."

"I hear you ate rats, bats, crows," Phillips said.

"You'd be surprised at what a person will eat when he's starving," Avery said.

"You heard Lee's orders?" Sykes asked.

"He surrendered," Avery said. "I know that much."

Sykes nodded. "He dismissed the army yesterday and told us to go to our homes and resume our occupations. He said we're to obey the law and become as good citizens as we were soldiers."

"From what I see," Phillips muttered, "there ain't no homes to return to, let alone occupations." For emphasis, he waved his arm at the burned farmhouse and unplanted fields to our left.

"I was told I was a good soldier for killing so many of the enemy." Sykes laughed. If a dead man could laugh he'd make the same sound. "You think Lee means I should go on shooting Yankees?"

"Fool." Phillips laughed and clapped his friend on the back, causing Sykes to start coughing again. "Ain't it great? With all he's been through, he ain't lost his sense of humor."

We walked on, conversing about the war. I was glad to see Avery sitting up straighter and taking notice, even talking a bit more than before.

By nightfall the four of us were fast friends. We built a campfire in the ruins of an old stone house and shared what little food we had. Dry cornbread, water, and a little chicory to make coffee. As usual, my belly felt emptier after I ate than before.

When the night turned chilly, we rolled up in our ratty old blankets. The men's talk turned to their homes, to wives and sweethearts and little children. Phillips was a married man, and he missed his wife and babies. Sykes had a pretty girl waiting for him down in Roanoke. Avery admitted he'd had his eye on a girl back home named Mary Alice Love, which was news to me, but he'd never had chance to do much courting. Just as he was working up the courage to kiss her, Papa had died, and he had run off to join the army.

"She'll be there when you get home," Sykes opined.

"Plenty of time for kissing then," Phillips put in with a laugh.

"With any luck a'tall, you'll find a preacher and a church still standing," Sykes added. "Why, this time next year you'll be a married man with a baby on the way."

I wanted to say something about Polly, but I was too bashful. Two kisses didn't count for much, I reckoned.

Gradually the men's voices faded. Sykes commenced to snore. Avery tossed and turned and muttered. Phillips ground his teeth. But I was too worried to sleep. I'd been counting on Avery for so long, and here he was lying beside me at last—a wreck of his former self, hollow-eyed, limping, too weak to work a farm. I truly hadn't expected him to be so changed.

The night turned colder. I curled up under my blanket in hope of finding warmth in my own breath, but the ground was cold and hard and damp. I couldn't find any comfort. Not in my body and not in my mind.

·22·

SOMETIME BEFORE NOON Sykes and Phillips left us to follow their own road home. Avery and I continued on toward Winchester. The roads were crowded with weary soldiers trudging home to farms and towns. Now and then we joined a group and traded stories. With some we shared campfires and food, sleeping together on the cold ground.

Once we stood on a muddy road in the rain waiting for a train full of Yankee troops to pass by. Most ignored us, but some leaned out the windows and jeered. We flung back insults as best we could, but they had the advantage of us. For one thing, they were dry. And they weren't walking to some far place like Indiana or Minnesota. No, the federal government was taking care of its own. We Southerners had to get home as best we could. For most of us that meant on foot.

One night when hunger kept Avery and me from sleeping, he asked me to tell him how Mama had died. It was hard telling that story, for I relived everything I spoke of. I saw the Yankees burst in upon us, and I watched Mama go upstairs with Captain Powell. I heard the pistol fire. I saw James Marshall's dead body hanging from the tree and heard the sound it made when I cut the rope and it fell to the ground. I went through Mama's sickness and death all over again.

"Mama killed a man?" Avery asked when I'd finished speaking. "Lord Almighty, Haswell, I can't imagine Mama with a gun in her hand, let alone pulling the trigger."

He began crying then, and I held him tight, doing my best to comfort him. Neither of us slept much that night.

Somehow we got ourselves up in the morning and kept going toward Winchester. By now most of the soldiers had taken different routes home and the roads weren't as crowded as they had been. Often folks would offer us eggs or bread or water. They always apologized for not having more. Then they'd ask if we'd seen their sons or husbands, their cousins, their friends.

"I'm hoping for word of my boy, Thomas Stone Noble," one might say. "He was in in the Army of Northern Virginia, Regiment B, Company Twelve. Tall, dark hair, real quiet but a good shot."

"You ain't run into Jefferson Tewkesbury, have you?" another might ask. "I ain't heard from him since Petersburg fell."

"My daddy was fighting with General Longstreet's men," a boy might tell us. "I'm hoping to see him come along any day now."

But there was never a name that Avery recognized. He'd sigh and shake his head.

"The Northern Virginia was a big army," he'd say. "I don't recall meeting a man by that name. But that doesn't mean anything. Just wait and pray. Some have a long journey home."

We'd go on our way, hoping their loved ones would soon return but knowing full well many of them were lying in shallow graves near the battlefields where they'd fallen.

As the days passed, I kept a close watch on Avery. He seemed to be recovering some of his strength, but he still complained of his head aching. He'd thrown his dirty bandage away, and I could see the saber's raw red line scoring his forehead from temple to temple. It looked as if the soldier wielding that saber had tried to slice the top of Avery's head off, the way you'd open a hard-boiled egg. It pained me to look at it.

Besides his head hurting, Avery was so stiff in the morning he needed me to help him stand up. He still asked for a boost onto Ranger's back, and he slept most of the day in the saddle, swaying back and forth like a drunkard.

Sometimes I'd catch him staring off into the distance, his eyes unfocused. I'd call his name and he wouldn't hear. It was as if his spirit had departed, leaving his body as slack as an empty grain sack. After giving him a shake, I could usually bring him back, but it worried me. What did he see? Where was he? If I asked him, he'd look at me blankly and shake his head. "What are you talking about, Haswell?"

That was as far as I could get with him.

On what must have been the ninth or tenth day, we came to a crossroads. The land looked familiar. The Blue Ridge Mountains were straight ahead, close enough now to see a green flush spreading across their slopes, softening the stark browns and grays of winter trees. Unplanted fields lay to the left and right.

I studied a weatherworn sign, tipped to one side but still standing. If we kept going straight, we'd be in Winchester by dark. I could scarcely believe we were so close to the end of our journey. With nothing but a sigh from Avery, I turned Ranger's head toward our uncle's home.

· 23 ·

AFTER A LONG, WEARY WHILE Avery and I entered Winchester. It was dusk on a chilly May evening. The sky threatened rain. Some of the war damage was hidden by weeds, vines, and shrubs coming into leaf, but here and there fireplaces and chimneys rose from blackened ruins.

A pair of men in Yankee uniforms strolled around a corner three blocks away. They were talking and laughing, but they were armed with rifles. The sight of them froze me in my tracks.

Avery looked down at me from Ranger's back. "What's troubling you, Haswell? You act as if we'd never seen Yankees before."

I tightened my grip on Ranger's reins. "Maybe I'm still wanted for horse theft. They could arrest me, put me in jail, hang me."

Avery sighed. "They're turning the corner, Haswell. I don't believe they have the slightest interest in either one of us."

Filled with misgivings, I made myself go on toward Uncle Cornelius's house. We passed raggedy people huddled around campfires in the ruins of their homes. A baby cried loudly in its sister's arms. The girl was no older than Rachel and hadn't the slightest idea how to hush the poor thing. The more she rocked it, the harder it cried. It was almost as if that little baby knew it had picked a bad time to be born.

When we reached Uncle Cornelius's street, I peered through the gloom, praying the house was still there. Now that I was this close, I was seized with a fear my family would be gone, driven away by war or sickness or death. What if I never saw Rachel again?

But my fears were for naught. The lawn was in worse condition than before, sprouting weeds and nettles and puddled with muddy water, but the house looked much the same.

After I took Ranger to the stable, Avery and I climbed the sagging steps to the front door. I lifted the tarnished brass ring in the lion's mouth and let it fall with a loud thud.

While we waited for a response, I noticed the door showed new scars of war. Chips, dents, smears of mud, what might have been bullet marks.

After knocking three or four times, we finally heard faltering footsteps approaching. "Who's there?" a voice called.

"Aunt," I called, "it's Haswell. Please open the door."

"Haswell!" Rachel shouted and noisily undid several bolts before flinging the door wide. She rushed out ahead of the aunts, but instead of giving us a warm welcome, she stopped short and stared past me at Avery. "Who's that man, Haswell? Why is he with you?"

"Why, that's Avery," I said. "Don't you remember your own brother?"

Rachel looked at Avery and shook her head. "Don't lie to me, Haswell. That's not Avery."

Avery stepped forward so the light from the hall chandelier illuminated his face. "I am most certainly Avery. Don't you know me?"

Rachel drew closer to me. "He doesn't look a bit like Avery."

I took her shoulders and gave her a little shake. "Lord, Rachel, mind your manners. He's been in the war all this time, with nothing to eat, sleeping in mud, fighting."

"What's that big red mark on his forehead?" Rachel stared at Avery's wound, clearly fascinated. She hadn't heard a word I'd said.

"A Yankee slashed him with his sword," I told her. "Almost killed him."

"It's true," Avery put in. "If I'd been any taller, he would have sliced my head clean off."

Rachel sucked in her breath and studied Avery more closely. He stood there patiently waiting for her to recognize him. At last she took a cautious step forward, then another. When he opened his arms, she ran into them. "Oh, Avery, Avery, of course it's you, of course it is." She hugged him so fiercely he tottered and grabbed the bannister to keep himself from falling.

The aunts rushed forward to hug Avery, too. While they exclaimed over his thinness, Rachel turned to me, her face flushed with anger. "It's about time you came back, Haswell Magruder. Why did you go off without me? It's been dreadful living here, just plain dreadful."

"I'm sorry, Rachel, truly I am." I gave her a hug, which I believe startled her, as I wasn't one to show much affection. "I missed you something terrible."

"You did?" Rachel had the look of a person struggling between belief and disbelief.

"Honest." I crossed my heart. It was more of an exaggeration than an outright lie, for I had missed Rachel, especially when I was alone or sick or scared. Other times I'd been too busy surviving to think of anyone else, including my family. But at the moment I was happier to see my sister than I'd believed possible in the old days.

"I gave you up for dead." Rachel's eyes filled with tears. "I thought I'd be living with Grandma Colby the rest of my days."

"Well, here I am, safe and sound." As I spoke, a little shiver ran up and down my neck, prickling the hair on my scalp. What if I wasn't safe after all? What if Major Dennison had left word that I was to be arrested for horse theft?

"Is anybody looking for me, Rachel?" I asked. "Am I wanted for horse theft or breaking out of jail or anything of that sort?"

Rachel gave me one of her squinty-eyed looks. "I've been mad enough to hang you ten times over for running off," she said. "But I highly doubt the Yankees give a hoot what happens to you. No matter what you think, you aren't all that important, Haswell." So saying, she tossed her head and turned her attention to Avery. I guess she believed she'd put me in my place, and I suppose she had. Nonetheless, I was mighty glad to hear my face wasn't on wanted posters all over town.

The aunts came up to me then and commenced to hug me and fuss over me till I thought I'd be smothered. Like Rachel, they'd never expected me to return alive.

"And to think you found Avery and brought him home safe," Aunt Hester exclaimed.

"We prayed every night for you both," Aunt Esther said. "It seems the good Lord heard our prayers." She turned her face up and stared at the ceiling as if she could see right through it, all the way to heaven. "Thank you, merciful Father, for sending Haswell and Avery home to us."

"Amen," Aunt Hester added solemnly.

"From the looks of you, I reckon you boys are starving." Aunt Esther took my hand and Aunt Hester took Avery's. With Rachel clinging to my other hand, we headed for the kitchen.

At the aunts' insistence, Avery and I took seats at the kitchen table. While the aunts stirred a kettle of stew already simmering on the stove, Rachel opened the oven and took out a sheet of biscuits.

"Just look at these, Haswell. I made them all by myself."

"Why, they look just as tasty as Mama's," I said. Rachel's face turned pink.

"I've learned to be a good cook," Rachel told Avery and me. "Isn't that so, aunts?"

"Yes, indeed," said Aunt Hester. "You'll be amazed at what that child can do."

"I don't know how we would have survived without her," Aunt Esther agreed. "Mother has been feeling too poorly to be of any help."

"And Corny has been a downright nuisance," Aunt Hester put in.

"Where *are* Grandma Colby and Uncle Cornelius?" I asked. "I thought they'd have come to greet us before now."

"Uncle Cornelius is most likely holed up in his library, having a glass of whiskey," Rachel said, "but Grandma Colby took to her bed when she heard of Lee's surrender. She claims she'd rather die than turn Yankee, but I think she just wants to be waited on."

"Now, Rachel," Aunt Esther said, "Mother is an old lady. She needs us to care for her."

"Yes," Aunt Hester agreed. "She cared for us when we were children, so we must—"

A bell on the kitchen wall jangled. "Oh, that's Mother now," Aunt Esther said, "wanting her supper."

Aunt Hester ladled stew into a bowl and set it down on a tray with Rachel's biscuits. Aunt Esther poured a cup of tea and set it beside the stew.

Handing the tray to Rachel, Aunt Hester said, "Please take this to your grandmother."

Without a word of protest, Rachel traipsed upstairs with the tray. It seemed Rachel's stay in Winchester had improved her attitude as well as her cooking skills.

She'd no sooner disappeared than Uncle Cornelius shuffled into the kitchen. He looked as if he'd aged ten years since I'd last seen him. His hair was almost white, and he leaned heavily on a cane.

"Lord Almighty," he muttered, "it's you, Haswell, come back to vex my old age. Though what else you can do to humiliate me lies beyond my imagining."

Before I had a chance to say a word, Uncle Cornelius noticed Avery. "Who the devil are you?"

My brother stepped forward. "I'm Avery Magruder," he said, "your sister Rebecca's son, just back from the war."

Avery held out his hand, but Uncle Cornelius was too busy fumbling in his pockets for a pair of spectacles to notice. After adjusting them on his nose, he peered more closely at Avery. "Oh, Lord, you and John, such handsome young fellows . . . and now, and now . . . "

His voice began to shake, and he turned his attention to the bowls Aunt Hester was setting on the table. "What's this? Carrots and potatoes again?"

"You should be glad to have it," Aunt Hester said.

"There's many a starving person in this town who'd eat it without complaining."

"For the love of heaven, don't start playing that tune again." Uncle Cornelius sat down heavily and stared into the fire burning on the kitchen hearth. "The war," he muttered, "I swear it's ruined me."

Rachel came downstairs and took a seat at the table. Ignoring her uncle, she began eating her stew.

Uncle Cornelius jerked his head in my direction. "I was doing fine until that boy came and disrupted my affairs. He turned the major against me. We haven't had a decent meal since the man left."

"Now, now, Corny." Aunt Hester went to her brother's side. "Calm yourself. You know what the doctor told you about agitating your heart."

"Major Dennison left our house because he was ordered into battle," Aunt Esther added soothingly. "It had nothing to do with Haswell's behavior. Nothing at all."

"I find I have lost my appetite." Uncle Cornelius rose slowly to his feet, leaving his food almost untouched, and turned away from the table.

"Where are you going, Corny?" Aunt Hester called after him.

"Please finish your meal," Aunt Esther implored.

Without looking at any of us, Uncle Cornelius left the room and made his way upstairs, thumping his cane on each step.

Except for Rachel's chatter, we finished our meal in silence. It wasn't the homecoming I'd hoped for, but I wasn't completely surprised. Uncle Cornelius had never been an easy man to talk to; even Papa had found him difficult. "Querulous" was his word for him, and easy to take offense. As for Grandma Colby, I was grateful she hadn't made an appearance yet, for she was bound to create a scene of some sort. The poor aunts looked worn out from trying to make peace.

I don't know how long we would have sat there if Grandma Colby's bell hadn't startled us into action. Aunt Hester scurried upstairs and soon came clattering down again.

"Haswell and Avery," she said, "Mother would very much like to see you."

Avery rose quickly, as if he still hoped for a warm welcome, but I wasn't eager to see Grandma Colby. I doubted she'd forgiven me for stealing a horse and disgracing the Colby name. Rachel followed us upstairs. Though no one had mentioned her, I reckoned she didn't want to miss the fireworks she was expecting.

· 24 ·

From her bed, Grandma Colby watched the three of us enter her room. She was propped up on pillows. A tall walnut headboard, carved with curlicues and flowers, towered above her. As Rachel had said, she didn't appear to be ill. Her eyes were as sharp as ever. I reckoned she meant to keep the Grim Reaper waiting a long while yet.

"Well," Grandma Colby said in a firm voice, "it seems the prodigal grandsons have returned after all. I never thought to see either of you again. Not in this world, that is."

Avery approached the bed and took Grandma Colby's bony little hand. "I'm glad to see you, ma'am," he said politely.

She nodded and peered past Avery at me. "Stop cringing in the doorway, Haswell. I haven't the strength to give you the beating you so roundly deserve."

I stepped forward reluctantly. "I never meant to shame you, ma'am," I said. "I didn't steal Ranger. Major Dennison had no right to him."

While the aunts, who had followed us up, took their places on either side of the bed, Grandma Colby sighed. "Well, I must say you did indeed mortify me, Haswell, but at least you showed the Colby spirit, standing up for yourself like that. Came to you from your grandfather, God rest his soul. He was a man among men. It's a good thing he's not here to see the state of the South today."

She fidgeted with the lace edging on her sheet. "For a while I feared you might take after your father's side of the family. The Magruders were always a spineless bunch, mooning over poetry and such, never much for action."

Beside me, I felt Avery draw his breath in hard, but before he could defend our father, Grandma eyed him sharply. "Don't you start talking about your brave deeds in battle, young man. The war never should have been fought. Anyone who indulges in such nonsense is a fool, whether he lives or he dies. Just look where fighting got us. Death and ruination everywhere."

She paused to cough into a lace handkerchief and then frowned at Rachel. "Take that thumb out of your mouth. You're seven years old. A young lady, not a baby."

Rachel removed her thumb and carefully wiped it on her dress.

"Just what are you doing in here anyway, Miss Nosy? Don't I see enough of you as it is?"

Rachel took my hand. Her thumb was still damp but I didn't snatch my hand away in distaste as I once would have.

Grandma Colby returned her attention to Avery and me. "What are you boys aiming to do now?"

Avery spoke right up. "Why, we'll go back to the farm, Grandma, and try to eke a living out of the land."

"I don't know how you'll do that. Hasn't Haswell told you the Yankees burned your house and barn and stole your livestock?"

"Yes, ma'am, he told me all about it." Avery straightened his shoulders. "But we'll manage. Magruders don't give up, no matter what the odds are."

"Is that right?" Grandma Colby eyed him coldly. It was clear she didn't agree with Avery's opinion of Papa's family.

"Yes'm," I put in. "Magruders have plenty of spirit."

Grandma Colby laid her head back on the pillows and gazed at the ceiling. "Well," she said without looking at anyone, "I reckon you'd better take yourselves down there and see for yourselves. As soon as Avery recovers, that is. Any fool can see he needs rest and food."

Rachel seized my hand. "Can we go home, Haswell? Can we?"

"You'd better stay right here, Rachel," Grandma Colby said. "Your brothers have men's business to tend to. They don't want a pesky little girl tagging along after them."

Rachel squeezed my hand tighter and drew in her breath to protest. Before she could say a word, Avery spoke up. "I think we need to be together, all three of us."

"Do as you wish," Grandma Colby said. "Magruders always have been as stubborn as mules." With that she closed her eyes and made it clear she wished to sleep.

Dismissed, we followed the aunts to the door. But Grandma Colby wasn't quite done. "For heaven's sake," she called after us, "take a bath before you sleep on my clean sheets. You boys are stinking up the entire house. It smells like a pig farm in here."

◊

As it turned out, Avery was in no shape to head for the farm any time soon. In fact, we ended up lingering in Winchester for almost a month to give him time to build up his strength. The aunts fed him as best they could and insisted he rest in the afternoons. Grandma Colby arose from her sickbed and oversaw Rachel and me, making sure we did all the chores she could think of. She had me chopping wood to last through next winter and making repairs to the steps and shutters and anything else that needed fixing, including an old buggy. Why she needed a buggy when she didn't own a horse to pull it was beyond my reasoning. But I did my best to restore it to working condition.

The old woman kept Rachel busy sewing and mending alongside the aunts. Every now and then Rachel stuck her finger with the needle. Grandma Colby gave her no sympathy, just fussed at her for getting blood on the linens.

Grandma Colby left Avery alone. Didn't make him do a thing. All day long he lay around reading books on agriculture. Sometimes he drew Uncle Cornelius into long conversations about the study and practice of law. Grandma Colby even told the aunts to make sure Avery had all the tea he wanted. Not that I minded. Avery had been through worse days than any of us. He deserved all the cosseting he could get.

Slowly the color returned to Avery's face. He was getting stronger, too. Though he still suffered fearsome headaches from his wound, he said they weren't as bad as they used to be. He smiled more and joked with the aunts, which pleased them no end. I guessed they'd never had much to laugh about living with Grandma Colby all those years.

At last the time came when Avery felt fit enough to set out for the farm. The morning we left, Grandma Colby loaned us the very buggy she'd made me repair.

"That child cannot possibly walk all the way home." To my surprise, the old woman gave Rachel a tender look, the first I'd ever seen her bestow on anyone. Then, as if she couldn't bear being soft, she added, "She's bound to dawdle and daydream and fuss. You'd never make it to the farm before nightfall."

I hushed Rachel with a tiny pinch. If she got sassy with Grandma Colby, the old lady might change her mind about the buggy.

The aunts gave us two loaves of fresh-made bread and apples from the fruit cellar, along with a jar of peach preserves and enough dried beans to see us through the summer. "I wish we had more to spare," Aunt Hester said.

Grandma Colby vanished into the house only to return a few moments later with Uncle Cornelius in tow, his arms filled with blankets. "Here," she said sharply. "Take these old things. We don't need them. They just attract moths."

Turning her attention to Rachel, she held up Sophia. "I believe you forgot this."

Rachel, her face flushed, grabbed the doll and hugged it to her chest.

"I swear to the Lord, you need someone watching over you every second of the day," Grandma Colby muttered. "You're so forgetful it's hard to believe you have a brain in your head."

Rachel hid her face in Sophia's dress and said nothing.

"You might thank me."

"Thank you, Grandma Colby," Rachel whispered.

The old woman sniffed. "That's all right, then."

With everyone watching, I harnessed Ranger to the buggy. It was clear he'd never pulled anything before and didn't care to start now, but I talked to him real soft. There were things that I hated doing, I whispered to him, like chopping firewood, but I did them anyway because it was my duty. Well, Ranger had a duty now and that was to pull a little old buggy so Rachel and Avery wouldn't get tired walking. It took me a while to persuade him, but finally he settled down and let me lead him a few steps.

"Good boy." Full of pride in his behavior, I stroked his nose. "I'll walk alongside you and keep you company every step of the way."

Ranger laid his ears back and gave me a skittish look, but he didn't balk. He was a darn fine horse. The best ever.

After powerful hugs and teary good-byes from the aunts, Rachel and Avery took their places in the buggy. Dry-eyed, Uncle Cornelius watched from the porch, raising his hand solemnly in farewell at an appropriate moment. Grandma Colby scurried about like a chicken, raising a cloud of dust as she shouted advice concerning everything from when to plant corn to how to break a horse to the plow.

By the time we finally left the house, I swear I could have lain down in the grass and slept till the next morning, I was that tired from all the commotion. But Avery and Rachel seemed eager to press on, so I roused my energy and kept going.

·25·

ONCE WINCHESTER LAY behind us, my spirits rose somewhat. Ahead was the winding road home, twisting in and out of forests and cutting between fields. If all went well, we'd be at the farm before dark.

The sun was warm on my back, and birds sang all around us. Wildflowers sprang up, splashing the tall grass with blue and red and yellow. Now and then a butterfly flew past my face, close enough for me to feel a flutter of air from its wings.

In the buggy Rachel chattered to Avery. She must have told him everything that had happened from the day he left till the day he returned. Every once in a while he asked her questions and she spouted answers. It seemed to me she strayed from the literal truth on more than one occasion, but I didn't call her on her embellishments. I figured Avery had the sense to know what was true and what wasn't.

While I trudged along beside Ranger, I felt the sun beat down on my head. It was the hottest day so far, one of those spells we get in springtime. The road was dusty. Soon my skin was gritty with sweat and dirt. Gnats circled my head, just waiting for me to stop so they could bite me. If I licked my lips, I could taste salt.

We'd taken the short way home, but it was still a long

journey. I had plenty of time to ponder what lay ahead. How would Avery feel when he saw the ruins of our farm? And what would we do about Mama and James Marshall? I dreaded the prospect of opening the springhouse door and seeing their bodies. I'd stumbled across enough dead soldiers to know how they'd look and smell. It turned my stomach to think of Mama and James Marshall lying there in the springhouse since February. Some things are best not seen or even imagined. I did my best to concentrate on the farm work that lay ahead, but my mind kept returning to the first task we'd face—burying Mama and James Marshall.

True to my guess, it was late in the afternoon when we rounded the road's last curve and stared up the hill at our farm. Our shadows slanted long and dark toward the house, like ghosts rushing home before us.

The chimney still stood. Vines had already begun climbing it, their leaves a vivid green against the rosy old brick. The mockingbird that always nested nearby perched there, singing his song.

Beyond the chimney, the mountain ridges rose one after another, almost transparent in the distance. The setting sun lit their wooded slopes, brightening the soft reds, golds, and greens of the leaves. Closer, the willow near the house lifted its long branches in a breeze. Its narrow leaves rose and fell like Mama's hair when she brushed it, swishing softly. Mama's lilacs bloomed and dandelions sprang up in multitudes, as if someone had scattered gold coins over the lawn.

"Oh, Lord," Avery whispered. "It's true. Papa's work and his Papa's before him—all gone, nothing left."

He urged Ranger forward. With me beside him, the

horse picked his way through ruts and puddles and muddy places.

"You say you left Mama and the soldier in the springhouse?" Avery asked.

I looked where he pointed. The springhouse door was open. The stones I'd put there lay scattered in the tall grass. My skin prickled all over with goose bumps. Had Rachel been right last winter? Had Mama waked up after we left and pushed the stones away?

Avery jumped out of the buggy, with Rachel behind him, her face lit with hope. I left Ranger to graze and hurried after them, longing to see Mama running toward us, arms flung wide to greet us.

But she didn't appear. I slowed to a stop behind my brother and sister. In this world the dead do not return to life.

From several feet away we stood and stared at the springhouse. Weeds had sprung up around it. Thistles and milkweed swayed in the breeze. Somewhere in the woods a crow called. Could animals have gotten into the springhouse?

"Stay here, Rachel," Avery said. "You, too, Haswell."

We did as he said, glad to let him do the looking.

Slowly Avery approached the open door. He hesitated a moment and then looked inside. Rachel held my hand with all her might, waiting.

At last Avery turned to us. "No one's here."

We looked at each other, puzzled. My throat and mouth were too dry to speak. Who would have moved Mama and James Marshall?

"Where can they be?" Rachel's eyes filled with tears, and she clung even more tightly to my hand.

Avery shook his head and gazed around him. Then, without a word, he strode off through the weeds. Rachel and I followed him. At the edge of the woods, he stopped. We were standing in the family burial ground, overgrown already with briars and vines and spiky thistles.

"There." Avery pointed to a new wood cross beside Papa's tombstone. Dropping to his knees, he brushed the weeds away. On the cross was Mama's name, carved as deep as a knife could cut. The earth was mounded over her body, not sunken yet like it was over Papa's grave.

While Rachel stared wordlessly at the cross, Avery turned to me. "Who did this, Haswell? Who buried Mama?"

"I don't know." I stared around in confusion. "Where is James Marshall? Why isn't he buried here, too?"

"Maybe someone found them in the springhouse," Avery speculated. "Someone who knew Mama but not James Marshall."

"He buried them both, but he didn't make a marker for James Marshall," I guessed.

We poked around in the weeds, looking for a fresh mound of earth, but there was no sign anywhere of a second grave.

"You suppose he's buried with Mama?" Avery asked.

"That could be," I said slowly.

Rachel tugged at my hand. "Remember that letter James Marshall wrote to his father?"

"What?" I stared down at my sister, genuinely puzzled.

"The letter you left in my room before you ran off to find Avery," she said.

So much had happened since then, I'd forgotten all about James Marshall's letter.

"Well, I did what you said," Rachel told me. "I wrote Mr.

Marshall how James Marshall died and where his body was. He must have come here to fetch him."

I looked at Rachel with new respect. "That must be it," I said. "But before he took James Marshall home, he buried Mama."

"That was a kind deed," Avery said thoughtfully. "We must thank him for it someday." He knelt down slowly, his legs stiff from riding in the buggy, and began to pray over Mama's grave.

Knowing he wanted privacy, I led Rachel back to the buggy and unharnessed Ranger. Glad to be free, he cantered across the field as if he were chasing his shadow.

While Rachel wandered through the tall grass picking dandelions and violets to put on Mama's grave, I went to the springhouse. The doors were open to the sunshine, and the spring water smelled clean and fresh. I filled a bucket for Ranger and another for us.

Rachel and I climbed down into the fruit cellar under the house. The air smelled of smoke and damp earth, but it seemed no one had used it for shelter during our absence. I supposed it was too well hidden by the ruins of our house to attract notice. The potatoes we'd left behind were moldering in an old basket, but we figured they were still edible.

While Rachel fetched more water from the springhouse, I got a fire going on the dirt floor. I built it near the door, hoping the smoke would blow outside.

Rachel stuck potatoes in the fire to bake. Just as I'd hoped, most of the smoke drifted out the door, but not all of it.

By the time Avery joined us, the sun had slipped behind the mountains and only a little light remained in the sky.

More silent than usual, Avery busied himself bringing

things from the buggy. The blankets were a welcome sight, for the evening air brought a chill with it.

"It was nice of Grandma Colby to give us these," I said, wrapping one of the blankets around my shoulders. "Do you think she's softening up a little?"

"She said they were old and she didn't want them," Rachel reminded me.

"Some people talk like that when they don't want to admit to doing a kindness," Avery told her. "Like remembering your doll and giving us the buggy so you wouldn't have to walk."

"Yes, but she claimed it was on account I'd dawdle and fuss." Rachel frowned at Avery. "She also said I didn't have a brain in my head."

It was clear Rachel wasn't ready to see much good in Grandma Colby. I guessed she must be too young to understand human nature the way Avery and I did.

I poked a potato out of the fire. "Here, Rachel, this one's done. Don't burn your fingers. It's hot."

We ate the potatoes silently. They had a musty taste, but we were too hungry and tired to complain. At least the aunts' bread was fresh, and the preserves were sweet and sticky.

When we'd finished eating, I grabbed a couple of apples and went to see Ranger. He was cropping grass, but he looked up when he heard me coming. I held out an apple, and he took it delicately with his big teeth. While he munched contentedly, I gazed past him at the mountains. In the dark, they looked like low-lying banks of cloud. I gave Ranger the second apple and rubbed my face against his. Then I left him to the starlight and ran back to the cellar.

To ward off the cold night air, we bundled up in our

blankets and huddled close together around the dying fire.

"Well," I said to Avery, "what should we do now?"

"What I said before," he answered. "Try to eke a living out of the land."

"How will we do that?" Rachel asked.

"We can start by cutting up the rest of the potatoes and planting them. They've all sprouted eyes," Avery said. "We also need to cut a smoke hole in the cellar roof so we don't choke to death. We'll be snug as rabbits in a burrow down here, even in the winter."

"Maybe we can scrounge up enough unburned wood to build a cabin," I suggested, thinking of Polly and Henry's home.

"Will we ever have a nice house again?" Rachel asked sadly.

"I don't know," Avery said. "The important thing is we've got each other. Even Grandma Colby says the Magruders are a stubborn bunch. We'll manage somehow."

"No matter how stubborn we are, it won't be easy," I said.

"No, it won't be easy," Avery agreed.

Rachel sighed and hugged her doll. "Sophia and I are tired," she said. "We don't want to talk about Hard Times anymore." With that she curled up in her blanket and closed her eyes.

Avery reached over and stroked Rachel's hair. "So pretty," he whispered, "just like Mama."

But Rachel was already sound asleep. Avery and I settled down beside her. For a while we reminisced about the old days before the war, laughing at things that happened long ago, family stories of the farm and our parents and the folks we'd known.

Avery dozed off first. While he snored softly, I stared into the fire, little more than glowing embers now. I wondered how Polly and Henry were and if the widow was treating them well. Someday I meant to ride down Farmville way and see Polly again. But that would have to wait a while. I had plenty of work to do here first.

In the gully the spring peepers were singing up a storm, their way of courting. An owl called, a fox barked, a mockingbird trilled a few notes. Ordinary sounds, sounds I'd heard all my life. I snuggled closer to Avery, safe at least for now. Hard Times lay behind me, Hard Times lay ahead. But at that moment, peace settled on me as gentle as moonlight shining on the mountains and fields of home.

About the Author

MARY DOWNING HAHN is a former children's librarian and the author of the Scott O'Dell Award novel *Stepping on the Cracks,* as well as numerous other critically acclaimed books for young readers. She lives in Columbia, Maryland.